ELEANOR

A REGENCY ROMANCE

MARTHA KEYES

To Brandon, Micah, and Jonah. You have helped me grow up in so many wonderful and important ways.

CHAPTER 1

*L*awrence Debenham set down his tankard with a small clank on the taproom table of The White Horse. He would only return home with three bottles of brandy—far less than he had intended to have from the innkeeper.

Had he known he would be returning home with barely half a crate full, he would have ridden his horse rather than bringing the carriage. He should have anticipated that Mr. Jeffers would be loath to part with his spirits when the area was filled to the brim with sporting men awaiting the start of the races.

The sound of raised voices outside the taproom met Lawrence's ears.

"But she is used to sleeping next to me," cried the insistent voice of a young boy. "She will have nightmares if she doesn't."

"Not on my property." The familiar voice of the innkeeper, Mr. Jeffers, was raised, as it so often was, and held a note of finality in it.

"Sir, if you please," the third voice belonged to a young woman, reasonable yet imploring, "I understand your hesitation. But she is very well-behaved. You shan't even know she's here. My brother is only five and cannot sleep without her, so I beg you to reconsider."

1

Lawrence's forehead wrinkled. Who was this "she" they spoke of? And why was she not permitted to stay in the inn?

"I have no rooms left to let," said Mr. Jeffers. "Perhaps you could try The Black Boar down the street. They are accustomed to accepting travelers of your caliber." His voice was laced with contempt.

Lawrence scoffed. A child and a lady putting up at The Black Boar? The man was intolerable. The innkeeper at The Black Boar was much more pleasant a fellow, but it was no place for anyone calling himself respectable. Definitely no place for a young woman or child.

"But I only just heard you tell a servant of an available room," the young woman said in exasperation.

"It has since been let," Mr. Jeffers said.

"What? In the two minutes since you said it? I am sure that we present a strange picture—my maid was sent on ahead of us a few days since—but I assure you that we are well able to afford a room."

Mr. Jeffers let out a derisive noise. "A likely story. Room or no, the three of you are not welcome at The White Horse."

"Humph!" said the boy. "Well, you are a very disagreeable man, and I don't like you."

"John," the scandalized voice of the young lady cried out.

Even through the door which was slightly ajar, Lawrence heard the boy let out a dramatic sigh.

"Fine," he said grudgingly, "I don't like you—sir." The last word was emphasized and drawn out.

Lawrence laughed aloud. Gad if the boy hadn't said what anyone had been wishing to say for ages. The innkeeper was disliked by everyone who frequented his inn. If he hadn't had such a fine collection of wines and spirits, Lawrence wouldn't have troubled himself with the place at all.

But the supply at Holywell House had dwindled, and Lawrence only trusted his own discriminating tastes to procure the best Jeffers had to offer. If Jeffers would only give up his supplier's name,

Lawrence could be rid of the innkeeper, but the man guarded his secret devilish close—no doubt to ensure the continuing patronage of people who would otherwise have nothing to do with him.

"Please forgive him, sir," said the young woman in a mortified voice. "He is tired from travel—I'm sure you can understand. But he will apologize." The last words were terse, and Lawrence could imagine the fiery look that accompanied them.

"I insist that you leave," Mr. Jeffers said abruptly.

"Please, sir," said the young woman, her voice desperate. "It's getting late, and we have nowhere else to go."

"Clowes!" Mr. Jeffers' voice rang out, calling for one of the servants. Rushed footsteps sounded. "Come escort these young persons off the property."

A slight scuffle ensued, and Lawrence, appalled at what he was hearing, stood and rushed to the door.

He looked at the scene before him, swiftly taking in the gangly form of Clowes, the ruddy-cheeked Mr. Jeffers, a young woman with her hand on the shoulder of the small boy next to her, and an enormous, long-haired black dog who panted happily with its tongue out. Lawrence stifled a smile at the realization that this dog was the "she" who Mr. Jeffers would not allow to sleep on the property.

Clowes's hand grasped the arm of the young lady, and she stepped back, disbelief and outrage written on her bonnet-framed face. Her angry eyes sparkled in a way Lawrence had never seen. He wondered if he should step in or if perhaps he would only cause offense in doing so.

"How dare you?" she cried, ripping her arm from Clowes's grasp and picking up the two leather portmanteaux at her feet. "We do not require an escort. Come, John."

She nudged her brother forward. He patted his thigh, bringing the dog to his side, then stuck out his tongue at the innkeeper—a gesture ignored by his sister—and the three of them walked out the door.

Mr. Jeffers brushed his hands off, his mouth turned down in

contempt and turned to walk toward the rear of the inn. Clowes stood in his way, though, and Mr. Jeffers was obliged to say, "Well? Don't you have things to attend to?"

Clowes scrambled to make way for his master then followed behind him.

Lawrence shook his head, wishing he could speak his mind to Mr. Jeffers as freely as the little boy John had done. What would the travelers do? Would they continue on to the next inn? There wouldn't be a room to be had for miles. Not with the races starting in a few days.

Lawrence stepped through the front door and into the carriage yard, hoping to warn them against The Black Boar and inform them that they would meet with similar news anywhere within 15 miles. There was no carriage in the yard, but the young woman, her brother, and the dog stood together, dimly illuminated by the sconces outside the inn.

"I was only being honest," said John defensively, "like you always tell me I must be."

His sister patted his shoulder. "I know, John." Her voice carried evidence of patience wearing down. "And in most cases, it is indeed best to be as honest as one can be, but surely you see how your honesty has put us in a bind? You heard Abrams—it will be a full two days before the wheel is fixed, and now we have nowhere to stay."

The boy sniffed, wiping a tear from his eye with the back of his hand. "I'm sorry."

She squatted down and put a hand on his little cheek. "Oh, John, don't be sorry. It is I who should be apologizing. I am sorry for being cross with you. We will come about somehow."

She stood up, looking across the road where the hedge-lined fields of gold-tinged green wheat were shrouded in darkness. Her shoulders slumped as she let out a large sigh.

Lawrence chewed the inside of his lip for a moment then straightened himself.

"Excuse me," he said, walking toward them. The dog barked

twice, and Lawrence stooped down to pet her, his hand disappearing in her thick, black fur. He looked up toward the young woman.

Her face was made visible by the light of the inn, and she was regarding him with a look both guarded and scrutinizing. From the front, Lawrence could see the honey-colored ringlets which framed her face beneath a chip straw bonnet. She was dressed tastefully but practically for travel, and it was obvious to Lawrence that she and her brother came from a family of decent means. She carried herself with a confidence he found foreign among his female acquaintances—it was sure without being arrogant.

"Don't mind Jeffers." He signaled behind him toward the inn. "He's just as abominable toward me, and I've known him for some time now."

John had been watching him with his head tilted to the side, and he stepped forward to join Lawrence in petting the dog, though his eyes stayed fixed on Lawrence.

"Do you have somewhere we can sleep?" John asked in a curious voice.

"John!" cried his older sister. "For heaven's sake!" She looked at Lawrence, her color heightened as she shook her head. "I apologize."

Lawrence laughed, pulling his hand from the depths of the dog's fur and looking John square in the eye. "I understand you're in a bit of a fix?"

John nodded. "We've nowhere to sleep because I was too honest."

Lawrence shot an amused glance at the young woman before responding. He clucked his tongue and shook his head. "Ah, honesty is a tricky thing, isn't it? And Mr. Jeffers dislikes it above anything. Perhaps it's for the best that you won't be staying here." He leaned in closer to John and whispered loudly, "He is a very stuffy man. Much too high in the instep."

The young woman stepped forward, her hands clasped in front of her as her thumbs twiddled. "He mentioned The Black Boar nearby?"

Lawrence stood up, shaking his head decidedly. "A fiendish suggestion. The Black Boar is nowhere you would care to set foot."

Her mouth twisted to the side. "I see."

He saw the anxious pull of her brow. "I would offer my carriage to take you to the next closest inn, but the devil's in it that you've happened upon the area just before the summer races at Newmarket. There's not a room to be had for miles. Where are you heading?"

The crease of her forehead deepened as she said, "To Attleborough. My father is there—only recently moved there."

Lawrence drew in a breath and shook his head. "That is a ways off, isn't it?"

"Well where are you staying?" John asked, his head tilted to the side again.

The young lady shot Lawrence an apologetic look, but he ruffled the boy's hair with a hand and said, "I live not far from here." He squatted down next to John and pointed north. "Just a couple of miles that way."

John leaned his head forward and squinted his eyes before shaking his head. "I can't see it."

Lawrence clapped him on the back as he stood. "That's all right. There's not much to see."

John humphed and turned toward Lawrence. "Well can't we stay with you?"

Lawrence's jaw slackened, and his eyes darted to the young woman.

Her eyes were wide in mortification. "Of course not!"

Lawrence looked down at the boy. He was looking up at him with wide, innocent, blue eyes. He liked the young fellow. But even more importantly, the two of them—or the three of them, if one counted the dog, which by all accounts one should since it was twice as large as John—were in a predicament with no apparent solution. He wondered if he would regret this.

"I think that's a brilliant notion," he said. "I only wish I had thought of it myself." He looked to John's older sister.

She was wringing her hands, her face conflicted. "It is very kind of you," she said slowly, "but we could not trouble you so. It would all be highly irregular."

Lawrence's brows went up, and he shrugged. "It is indeed irregular, but your situation is highly irregular, is it not? Did I correctly gather that you are awaiting the repair of a carriage wheel? In addition to having a massive dog which no landlord is likely to tolerate even if there were a room to be had in the vicinity which, I can assure you, there is not."

"Don't be a ninny," said John to his sister as he brought a hand to cover a large yawn. He motioned for the dog to get up and looked to Lawrence. "Where is your carriage?"

Lawrence's mouth twitched, and he looked at the young woman. She was watching John with a worried expression as he stifled yet another yawn. She bit her lip.

"There is room and to spare at my estate," Lawrence said, hoping to allay her fears. "It would be no trouble at all, I assure you. I was just about to leave, myself. And my carriage would be at your disposal, should you care to return to town in the morning."

John's voice piped in. "You won't make Anne sleep outside, will you?" Slight suspicion was written on his face.

Lawrence's eyes shifted toward the young woman.

"Anne is the dog," she explained.

"Ah," he said with a slow nod and a half-smile. "Perhaps to avoid any further confusion, we should introduce ourselves? I am Lawrence Debenham, at your service." He tipped his hat.

She opened her mouth but was cut off by John.

"My name," he said, pushing out his chest, and speaking with fierce pride, "is Johnathan Michael Renwick. But you can call me John. And this is my sister, Eleanor. But we just call her Nell."

Mr. Debenham nodded formally, though his mouth twitched. "Delighted to make your acquaintance." He reached down to the dog and shook its paw. "And yours, Anne." He looked back up to Miss Renwick. "I understand your hesitation, Miss Renwick, and if I thought there were another, more suitable option for you, I assure you I wouldn't hesitate to tell you of it. But I hope you will allow me to be of help to you in your unfortunate situation."

Miss Renwick was looking at the dog and drew in a deep breath before letting it out slowly. "It is very kind in you," she said, rubbing her lips together, her hands still clasped nervously in front of her. "We would be very grateful for your assistance and will do our best not to be a burden upon you."

Lawrence glanced at John who was engaged in practicing a hand-shake with the dog, instructing her with a stern voice on the proper method. Lawrence flashed a grin at the young woman. "A burden? Rather a welcome distraction, I think."

CHAPTER 2

*E*leanor Renwick sat in the carriage with her arms folded, a finger tapping nervously as she waited for the gentleman to return from the inn so that they could start their journey. He had been kind enough to offer to leave a message with the innkeeper so that the coachman would know where to find them once the repairs were done. John sat next to her, staring out the carriage window with lids that were beginning to droop. The large Newfoundland dog lay contentedly at John's feet, taking up almost the entirety of the carriage floor.

Eleanor had grave doubts about the wisdom of the course they were taking, but what other choice did they have? She had done everything she could think of to prepare for the journey to their new home—planning out their stops with meticulous care, ensuring that the majority of their belongings left with her maid a few days before.

But she had never considered the possibility of a broken carriage wheel, nor had she realized that they would be traveling into a region at one of the few times of year when it was overrun with sporting men. Sending the maid on before them now seemed a reckless choice rather than a prudent way of helping reduce her father's burden.

She was grateful to Mr. Debenham. He had spared them from the prospect of sleeping out of doors or, equally mortifying, going from door to door in the unknown village requesting pity and a room for two nights as they awaited the mending of their carriage wheel.

She had sensed by his genuine smile and kind eyes that he was trustworthy, and his kindness to John had given her a needed boost of confidence in his character. Knowing that Anne would protect them if she sensed the need had given Eleanor the final reassurance she needed to accept Mr. Debenham's help.

But his generosity did not change the fact that they would be lodging with a stranger, one who seemed by all accounts to be a bachelor. That he was more handsome than any gentleman of Eleanor's acquaintance did nothing to allay her qualms. Her reputation was at stake, she knew. She could only hope that the brevity of their stay and the low probability of ever crossing paths with anyone in the town would protect her from potential problems.

She was relieved that at least she would not be obliged to write her father to inform him of the mishap. She had given him a range of likely days for their arrival, and a delay of two days would put them within that range—on the tail end, but within it, all the same. Anything she could do to relieve some of his burden, she would do gladly. He had been through enough trying to ready the house for their arrival—he didn't need an extra reason to worry.

She hoped that the novelty of the home was shaping up to be the blank slate he so desperately needed and that the arrival of her two siblings from their respective schools would distract him from his troubles. Roger and Henry had a way of raising their father's spirits with nothing but their company.

It was hard to imagine that two years of intense grieving wouldn't soon give way to some peace. She had to believe that it would. John had gone far too long with a father whose mind and heart were unreliable and frequently absent. It was hard enough to lose a mother, but sometimes it felt just as difficult to see their father physically present but absent in every other way.

The carriage door opened, bringing her out of her abstraction. Mr. Debenham stepped in with a wooden crate under his arm. The bottles inside it clanked lightly as he moved. He paused for a moment on the threshold, looking down at the mass of dog covering the floor, and then gingerly stepped in a small open spot.

"Ah," he sighed, taking a seat and resting the crate next to him. "Let's be on our way, then, shall we?" He knocked on the carriage roof, and they jolted forward.

Anne's head perked up for a moment before it returned with a thump to its spot on the floor. Mr. Debenham examined the large lump of fur before him. "I admit that I find Anne a strange name for a dog. I have a sister named Anne, you know."

"Hm," John said curiously, tipping his head to the side. "Which pirate is your sister named after?"

Mr. Debenham's eyebrows went up, and he seemed to stifle a laugh.

"Anne isn't only a name for pirates, John," Eleanor said in a practical voice. She looked at Mr. Debenham and smiled. "John is very taken with the idea of pirates, hence the name of the dog. She is named after Anne Bonny, the Irish pirate."

Mr. Debenham nodded slowly, saying, "Ah, I see." He looked to John. "And which pirate did you understand my sister to be named for?"

John shrugged his shoulders. "Perhaps after Anne Dieu-le-Veut? She was impressive, but she could never compare to Anne Bonny, of course."

"Decidedly not," said Mr. Debenham gravely, shaking his head. He paused, clasping his hands in his lap. "And why can she not compare?"

"She was captured," said John simply.

"How very careless of her," said Mr. Debenham. "But was not Anne Bonny also captured?"

"Of course not!" John said contemptuously.

"John," said Eleanor, admonishing him. "That is not true, you know."

"Well it doesn't count! She escaped," he reasoned. Eleanor glanced at Mr. Debenham who was looking at her in mock censure in support of John's words. His eyes danced, though.

Eleanor shook her head. "We don't know if she escaped, John. No one knows for sure."

"I'm sure of it!" John cried, and his mouth turned down as though he might start crying.

Mr. Debenham clenched his teeth, and Eleanor raised her brows in a long-suffering gesture.

"You know, John," Mr. Debenham said, leaning across the carriage to confer with him, "I believe you're right. I've heard tales of her ghost. They say it haunts any ship with gold aboard."

John's eyes grew round. "Really?"

Mr. Debenham nodded. "I will tell you a tale or two, but you must swear to keep them secret."

John nodded quickly, sitting on the edge of the seat as Mr. Debenham began telling the tales in a hushed voice, the carriage bobbing up and down all the while.

Eleanor smiled and leaned back in her seat, her eyes moving back and forth between her brother and Mr. Debenham. John leaned forward in his chair as if he couldn't bear to miss a single word. The yawning from earlier was long gone—he was in his element.

Mr. Debenham's hands were expressive and his face even more so. How fortunate that they had happened upon a gentleman both willing to accommodate them and one learned in pirate lore.

When the carriage pulled into the courtyard of Mr. Debenham's estate, Eleanor's relaxed state—brought on by listening to his entertaining pirate tales—was replaced by a fresh wave of anxiety. Eleanor was still unsure what to expect. She was fairly certain that Mr.

Debenham was not married, but if he was, how would his wife react to her uninvited guests? Particularly the enormous dog.

Mr. Debenham exited the carriage first, extending a hand to help Eleanor down. John wanted no assistance, though, and hopped down energetically, calling to Anne to follow. The dog was not quite so deft in her exit, and Mr. Debenham was obliged to assist her.

Eleanor bit her lip as she watched. She had hoped to be inconspicuous guests, but the likelihood of that seemed to decrease by the minute. Mr. Debenham removed the two portmanteaux and his crate from the carriage and led them toward the house. John seemed very taken with him and followed on his heels as closely as Anne followed on John's.

The estate was poorly-lit from the outside. Only two sconces on either side of the front door illuminated the house, their light fading into deep shadows among the surrounding ivy. Mr. Debenham opened the door himself, leading them into an entry hall equally as poorly-lit as had been the exterior. The muffled sound of men's voices met Eleanor's ears, and her stomach lurched as she wondered what kind of situation she had led herself and her young brother into.

"Ah," said Mr. Debenham, setting down his load on the floor. "I should perhaps have informed you that I have two friends staying here. But don't worry—they are quite harmless."

Eleanor forced a smile and looked down at John who was yawning.

"I would have the housekeeper show you to a room," Mr. Debenham said, "but the truth is that I gave her the night off. I only keep a couple of servants on—a housekeeper and the man who acts as a sort of driver, footman, and butler. I have yet to hire a full staff. The two I do have tend to all my needs which are few. But I will be glad to show you upstairs."

He reached for an unlit candle on a nearby table, lighting it using one of the sconces on the wall.

The three of them trod up the stairs, followed closely by Anne. The upstairs hallway was shrouded in darkness, and Eleanor couldn't help feeling anxious. It was difficult to tell for certain in the obscurely-lit hallway, but the smell of dust was strong, and the house seemed in need of repairs. If it weren't July and too warm for a fire, she would worry, too, about the chimney smoking.

John's lungs had never fully recovered from his bout of whooping cough shortly after their mother's death. Eleanor had sat with him for three weeks, catering to his every need, listening as the cough dissipated over time, only to be agitated by the smoke from the fire in his room. Eleanor had arranged for the nursery to be moved, and he had been much better with only a few instances of coughing since.

Mr. Debenham led them through a door off the hallway, and the candle cast moody shadows as he moved through the room and set it down on the bedside table.

"I'm afraid this is the only vacant room at the moment," he said with a frown. "At least, it's the only one not shrouded in holland covers. Tomorrow night Mrs. O'Keefe—she's the housekeeper—can make up a bed in one of the other rooms. For tonight, I shall just go fetch your portmanteaux and more blankets. Perhaps John can sleep on the floor?"

Eleanor looked to John, but his eyes seemed to be fixed on the walls of the room. Eleanor followed his gaze to the large shadows cast all over the room. Was he scared? "John?" she said, putting a hand on his shoulder.

He jumped slightly.

"Mr. Debenham was just saying that we can make a bed for you on the floor. Is that all right?"

John's eyes were wide as he looked at Mr. Debenham and then to Eleanor. "And you will sleep in the bed?"

She smiled at him and nodded, and his shoulders seemed to relax. She glanced at Mr. Debenham whose lips were pursed as he watched John.

John looked to him and said, "Mr. Deneban—Demeban." He grunted in frustration.

Mr. Debenham suppressed a smile. "Devilish name, isn't it? You may call me Lawrence if you wish, though."

"What about Lawrie?"

Mr. Debenham's mouth opened wordlessly.

"John," Eleanor said in a censuring tone.

John looked at her and folded his arms across his chest. "What? I hate long names! I go by John; you go by Nell—why should he not go by Lawrie?"

Mr. Debenham had his arms folded, and a hand covered his mouth. He looked at Eleanor with a significant glance and said, "A home question." He turned to John. "Lawrie it is!" He clapped John on the shoulder and then excused himself to retrieve the blankets.

Eleanor knew she should be more embarrassed at her brother's behavior, but her fatigue was severe enough to keep those emotions at bay. Whatever regrets Mr. Debenham might come to feel about offering them his home, they would be nothing more than a strange memory in two days when the Renwicks continued on their way.

For now, though, Mr. Debenham's response to John's forthright and uninhibited dialogue was a relief. He seemed to take it all in stride, finding it amusing rather than offensive or off-putting. Eleanor couldn't help but feel that, despite her hesitations, they had been unduly fortunate in happening upon a gentleman who seemed so agreeable and forbearing.

CHAPTER 3

*J*ohn stood next to the candle, placing his fingers near it and watching the way the shadows fell onto the wall behind.

Eleanor smiled slightly. "Be careful not to burn yourself or tip over the candle. We must be on our very best behavior, John. We are intruding upon Mr. Debenham, and we must try to make the imposition as painless as possible for him. Particularly since he seems to be entertaining friends."

John nodded absently, twisting his fingers into a new shape and smiling at the effect. Eleanor sighed. It was useless to reason with him.

When Mr. Debenham returned, his arms were stacked high with the portmanteaux and a heap of blankets, on top of which a pillow was teetering precariously. Eleanor rushed over as he came through the doorway, catching the pillow as it slid off.

"Ah," Mr. Debenham said, lowering the heap onto the floor. "Thank you. This should keep you comfortable, my good man."

John looked at the mass of blankets with wide eyes and then took a few steps back. Eleanor observed him with a creased brow. What he saw to trigger fear in a pile of blankets was a mystery.

Her eyebrows shot up as she watched him run the few steps between him and the blankets and then jump onto the pile. Muffled giggles sounded from the center of the mass where John's face was buried. Eleanor was half-embarrassed at her brother's wild behavior, half-relieved to know that what she had mistaken for fear was simply awe. She looked over to Mr. Debenham who was wearing a wide grin.

He bent his knees, brought one leg back and then jumped onto the pile, crying, "Yo ho ho!"

John was ecstatic at finding that Mr. Debenham had followed his example, and for some time, the two of them scuffled inside the blankets, throwing the pillow at one another while Eleanor looked on, amused and mystified. The transformation of Mr. Debenham from proper gentleman to childish pirate was entirely unexpected and equally entertaining.

She finally snatched the pillow from John's hands.

"We really must get you to bed, John," she said, plumping the pillow. "It is far past your usual bedtime."

When he and Mr. Debenham stood, their hair was disheveled, a fact which John seemed not to mind. Mr. Debenham ran a hand through his, but a few pockets were left standing up. Eleanor's mouth quivered as he stood in front of her—any intimidation she had felt since meeting him was successfully quelled by the figure he presented.

John's face pouted. "But I don't want to go to bed."

"Why ever not?" said Eleanor. "You will be so terribly comfortable, surrounded by all these blankets."

John sent a side-eyed glance at Mr. Debenham and then walked over to Eleanor and leaned toward her. He shot another glance at Mr. Debenham who seemed to gather that he was not the desired recipient of John's confidences and busied himself with placing the pillow at the top of the blanket Eleanor had spread out.

"I am," John said in a half-whisper to his sister, "frightened of this place. It's so dark. And there are cobwebs."

Eleanor shot a quick look at Mr. Debenham who, though his hands were busy, appeared to have heard John's words. Eleanor knew that John was rather particular about how he fell asleep and that he had never slept anywhere but the London house and the house in Kent. This experience was entirely new to him.

She put a hand on his shoulder and kneeled down in front of him. "It is very different here than you are used to, isn't it?" She thought of the light-colored wallpaper and various candles which normally lit John's room at night. After John was fast asleep, one of the servants would extinguish the two he insisted on keeping lit while he dozed off.

The single candle in this room only accentuated the moody hues of maroon and brown on its peeling, papered walls. Eleanor wondered how recently Mr. Debenham had taken up residence. Given the presence of only two servants and the disrepair she had seen in the short time they had been there, it seemed he must have only just arrived.

John nodded. "Yes, very different."

"But different doesn't mean bad, you know. Sometimes it is a good thing, in fact."

John looked doubtful. "But what about the Colonel?"

Eleanor stood and smiled, walking over to one of the portmanteaux which she opened and then sorted through, pulling from it a toy soldier. John looked over at Mr. Debenham surreptitiously as he approached Eleanor to take the toy, as though he was afraid the gentleman might think ill of him.

Mr. Debenham seemed to sense that his reaction was of importance to the child, and he said, "Ah, so this is the good colonel?" He walked over to John and then saluted the toy soldier with all the gravity of one of the King's officers.

John giggled, and Eleanor breathed a sigh of relief. She took another blanket from the pile, throwing it gently over the other.

"And now that you have the Colonel," she said, "you may ready yourself for bed."

The smile faded from John's face, but on meeting Eleanor's stern look, he removed his jacket and shoes.

"I'm afraid," Eleanor continued, "your night clothes went on ahead with the rest of our belongings a few days ago, so you will simply have to sleep in what you have on."

John sighed melodramatically, and Eleanor looked at him from the corner of her eye with a slightly amused smile. She took the pillow and fluffed it. "What a luxurious pillow! Fit for a king. I hope you did not take it from your own bed, Mr. Debenham?" She lifted the top blanket, helping John slide into the makeshift bed.

"No, no," said Mr. Debenham with a quick head shake. "We have plenty on hand." He glanced over at Anne who was sprawled out on a rug in the corner of the room. He cleared his throat. "Does, uh, Anne require anything?"

John laughed. "No, silly! She is already asleep." He tilted his head, looking at Anne who was barely discernible by the flame of the small candle. "It seems dreadfully uncomfortable." He looked at Mr. Debenham. "Perhaps a pillow would be good." He said it as if he were instructing a servant, and Eleanor's eyes widened.

"John, good heavens!" she said. "Anne is perfectly fine where she is. She has no need of a pillow." She shot an apologetic glance at Mr. Debenham who looked politely interested to discover whether he should be required to fetch a pillow for the dog after all.

John sniffed, looking sideways at Eleanor with an unhappy expression. "But she does need a pillow! Else she will snore so loudly that I can't sleep a wink. She always has a pillow at home."

He looked to be on the verge of tears, and Eleanor felt her temper fraying. John was being much more difficult than he usually was—and he had always been an obstinate child.

"Well," Mr. Debenham chimed in, "we can't have snoring! If there's one thing I can't abide, it is a snoring dog. I shall fetch another pillow post-haste."

Eleanor clenched her teeth, wishing she could spare him the trouble, but Mr. Debenham only winked at her as he strode out the door once again.

Eleanor suppressed an urge to berate John, telling herself that he was only being difficult because he was anxious in his new environment. At home he had demanded Eleanor for much of his care, but she had always been able to fall back on the nurse at need. Being solely responsible for him as they traveled had given her a new appreciation for the energy John's care required.

He called Anne to come over, and the dog heaved herself up obediently, trudging toward him with droopy eyes and plopping down next to him on the floor. He rubbed her ears for a moment before laying back down into his pillow and rearranging the Colonel to be at its side.

Mr. Debenham tripped into the room with another pillow in hand. He noted the dog's new position next to John and raised a brow at Eleanor who only shrugged resignedly.

Mr. Debenham bent down and offered the pillow to John. "A pillow for Anne—one fit for a pirate, I think."

Eleanor bit her lip. The pillow was not nearly as full as John's was, and it looked the worse for wear, with various stains and a distinct lumpiness to it. It was precisely the type of pillow fit for a dirty dog like Anne.

John looked at it askance. "Hmm...it is not very nice, is it?"

"I believe," Eleanor said, talking over John, "that what my brother means to say is 'thank you.' Isn't it, John?" She looked at him with a threatening smile.

John looked at her for a moment and then to the pillow before saying in a glum voice. "Thank you, Lawrie." He lifted Anne's head and slid the pillow under it, then dropped down onto his own, looking up at the ceiling where the flickering candlelight danced.

Eleanor shot a look of long-suffering at Mr. Debenham who, much to his credit, only looked amused. She sent a silent prayer of thanks to the fates who had placed her and John in this good-natured man's hands. "Thank you very much. We owe you a great debt of gratitude."

Mr. Debenham waved a dismissive hand. "Nonsense. You owe me nothing at all." He looked around the room and then back at Eleanor. "Is there anything I've forgotten? I don't wish you to be uncomfortable."

Eleanor shook her head quickly as she thought of the type of night she and John would have faced without Mr. Debenham's assistance. "No, we shall do very well. Much better, mind you, than if we had been obliged to seek accommodation at The Black Boar."

Mr. Debenham's side smile appeared. "I certainly hope so."

"I can't seem to fall asleep," came John's small voice. He still lay staring up at the ceiling, but his eyes held a glint of fear in them. His arms were on top of the blanket, his clasped fingers twiddling.

Eleanor's mouth twisted to the side. "John, my dear, you haven't been in bed above two minutes. Of course you haven't been able to fall asleep yet. Once I snuff the candle, I'm sure you will do just fine."

"No," cried out John, sitting up straight with wide eyes.

Mr. Debenham had been moving toward the door but stopped in his tracks at the outburst. His head tilted to the side, and he looked at Eleanor with a question in his eyes.

She returned his glance with her own confused expression then walked over to her brother, crouching down next to him. "What is it?"

He eyed the candle dubiously. "Don't snuff it out, please." His eyes flitted to Mr. Debenham, and he spoke in a whisper when he said, "It's too dark."

Eleanor sighed. If John refused to fall asleep without candlelight, she would be obliged to wait to snuff it until he was soundly asleep, putting off her own rest even longer when she was already exhausted.

"Shall I tell you a story, then?" Eleanor said. Their mother had been a wonderful storyteller, and though John had been very young when she had died, he still spoke from time to time of the stories she told. Neither Eleanor nor her father had the same knack for weaving

21

tales, and with time, John seemed to accept that his bedtime would no longer include anything but a few stories Eleanor had memorized.

"I hate your stories," John said, folding his arms obstinately. "You always tell the same ones over and over."

Mr. Debenham was standing near the door, and he seemed to be torn between staying and leaving. John looked at him out of the corner of his eye, and his shoulders suddenly relaxed.

"Lawrie," he said. "Will you tell me a story?"

Mr. Debenham's mouth opened and then shut, and he looked at Eleanor who felt her cheeks heating up. John seemed determined to make Mr. Debenham regret bringing them into his home.

The muted sound of laughter met their ears, and Mr. Debenham glanced at the door.

"John," Eleanor said, "Mr. Debenham is entertaining guests. He can't possibly leave them to fend for themselves just to tell you a story, love. Tell him thank you and good night."

Eleanor watched as John's eyes moved to Mr. Debenham. They were round and so pathetic as to be endearing. "Thank you, Lawrie. And good night." His words were just as she had asked them to be, but his eyes begged Mr. Debenham.

Mr. Debenham didn't move, staring at John with his lips working for a moment. "Once upon a time," he finally said, walking from the door toward John's makeshift bed. He sat down on the floor next to the dog, leaning his back against the large, wooden bed frame, one hand in his lap, the other lost in Anne's fur. John propped himself up on his elbow, his eyes sparkling with excitement.

Eleanor tried to catch Mr. Debenham's eye—to send him a look of gratitude, since that was all she could do to thank him in the moment —but he wasn't looking at her. How could she ever thank him for his generosity? And when would it peter out? For it surely would by the time they left in two days if John persisted in making a hero out of the man.

"John," Eleanor interrupted, "if Mr. Debenham is to tell you a story, you must lie down while you listen and promise to make no complaints when I snuff out the candle afterward."

John nodded solemnly and laid down on his side, resting his head on his hand with the pillow underneath.

"Once upon a time," Mr. Debenham continued, "there was an old, mossy ship, washed up on the shore off the coast of Cornwall. The wood was rotting, the sails were tattered, and the paint on the side had faded so that you could barely see the name of the vessel: Neverland.

"For years it sat on the rocky beach, but no one dared go in. Legend has it that it washed ashore in the middle of the night during a winter storm, full of pirates and their treasure—gold and jewels and pearls and silks—" his hands made grand gestures with each word "— the likes of which you and I have never seen." He stopped, and John's wide eyes stared, waiting for more. "Only one man witnessed the shipwreck, but he disappeared the day after, never to be heard of since. His name was William. This is his tale."

Eleanor blinked twice. She realized that she was leaning forward slightly, waiting upon Mr. Debenham's words with almost as much anticipation as John. She smiled. Even when she herself had become too old for bedtime stories, she would often sit on the edge of John's bed and listen as their mother created a new tale, night after night. She hadn't realized how much she missed those evenings and the calming sound of her mother's voice as she listened with a shawl wrapped around her shoulders and the fire in the grate warming her back.

She sat down on the floor, her back against the wall and her legs tucked to the side. Mr. Debenham's story carried on, and Eleanor watched him—the boyish excitement in her brother's eyes was reflected back at him in Mr. Debenham's. A lock of his sandy hair had dropped onto his forehead. He looked every bit as youthful as John did. He was in his element.

Eleanor watched with a small smile as John's eyelids started to droop, only to fly open as he tried his hardest to stay awake. But his exhaustion won out in the end, attested to by the small drop of saliva pooling at the side of his mouth. Eleanor's head tipped to the side, and she let out a breath of relief.

Her eyes flitted to Mr. Debenham who was regarding her with a thoughtful expression. He put a shushing finger to his lips and gingerly raised himself off the ground, baring his teeth as he watched John for any sign of disturbance. The effort was met with success, though, and John remained as he had been for the last few minutes, except for the saliva which slid down his chin and dripped onto the pillow below.

Eleanor stifled a laugh with her hand, raising herself from the ground as softly as she could manage. Mr. Debenham offered her his hand and helped her up. They walked to the door, and she was aware of a sudden shy feeling. With John asleep, she felt very much alone with her host.

"You have been far too accommodating and kind," she said in a whisper, keeping her eyes on John—to watch for any signs of waking, but also to avoid looking Mr. Debenham in the eye.

Mr. Debenham leaned in closer, his ear toward her. "What was that?"

She clenched her teeth, afraid to speak any louder. He grimaced his understanding and pulled the door open slowly, inviting her with a nod of his head to step out. She swallowed nervously, hesitant to follow, but she felt a pressing need to express her gratitude to him.

He left the door ajar once they were out of the room, a fact which Eleanor noted and appreciated, as it allowed at least a few beams of candlelight into the otherwise-dark hallway.

"I was only wishful to thank you," she said, clearing her throat, "for your attention and kindness to us. You have gone above and beyond anything I expected or could have asked for. I wish I could find a way to repay you, and I am terribly sorry if you are already regretting your—"

He put up a hand to silence her, and she stopped.

A small smile appeared on his face, and he put his hand down awkwardly. "I apologize," he said. "That was impolite of me. But I'm afraid I have never been very good at accepting thanks. I am only glad that I've been able to provide some assistance."

"Some assistance?" Her brows went up. "That is a gross understatement, sir. But I shan't continue with my thanks if it would make you uncomfortable."

"Thank you," he said, with a sigh of relief.

Her mouth curved up on one side. "Ah, so you are permitted to express your thanks but I am not? I see." She nodded in teasing comprehension.

He pursed his lips. "Touché."

She glanced through the crack in the door where she could see John lying peacefully. The Colonel was nestled in the crook of his arm.

"Your story was precisely what John had hoped for. It has been a great while since he's been able to enjoy such a well-crafted bedtime story."

Mr. Debenham shook his head with a pained expression. "It was a silly choice on my part. I made it far too exciting for a lad needing to fall asleep—I realized that about halfway through and made sure to dampen the excitement to a level more conducive to boredom."

"Whatever you did," she said, "it worked. I was dreading the battle of getting him to sleep. He has struggled since our mother's passing—she used to tell him bedtime stories every night. Wonderful creations, much like yours."

How many times had she wished for her mother's presence on those late nights when John would toss and turn, refusing everyone but herself? John had been young enough when their mother died that not even he realized why he couldn't sleep. But Eleanor knew. And yet she felt helpless.

She turned to look at Mr. Debenham and smiled feebly. "Unlike you, I am not favored with a creative mind. John hasn't hesitated to inform me that my repetitive, memorized stories leave much to be desired."

Mr. Debenham looked at her with a slight crease between his brows, his eyes staring into hers as if he were seeing her for the first time. "Everyone has a creative mind."

She laughed softly. "That you should say that is only more evidence of your imagination. Some of us are purely practical. You would believe me if you had heard me tell a story."

He shook his head. "You have simply forgotten how. A child's mind is always creating. It is only when we grow up that we forget how to create."

Eleanor stood in silence. She had indeed grown up quickly. There had been little choice in the matter. Her mother's illness had started subtly. And just as subtly, it had begun to require more and more of Eleanor until her mother's death had extinguished the last flicker of childhood.

When she had donned her blacks, Eleanor had put away plans and hopes as if in the back of a drawer. She no longer had use for such things.

"And what of you?" she said, coming out of her reverie. Who was this man who seemed to be free enough from sorrow that he could still create as a child does?

Mr. Debenham's gaze moved from her eyes into the inky hallway beyond. His jaw went hard. "There are enough adults in my life and to spare."

Eleanor blinked, surprised by the sudden shift in his tone.

He looked at her and blew out a laugh. "Have no fear. We will revive your imagination yet, Miss Renwick."

Eleanor swallowed, suddenly aware of the small distance between them despite the entire length of the vacant hallway available. Her impulse was to take a step back, but she feared giving offense.

Mr. Debenham must have sensed her unease, as he bowed his head slightly and said, "I am sure you are exhausted from your journey, and here I am, keeping you from rest."

Eleanor shook her head quickly. "No, not at all. You have been nothing but helpful and kind to us."

"Well," he said, glancing toward the dimly-lit form of John through the crack in the doorway, "please don't hesitate to call upon me if you have any need at all."

He bowed again, turning on his heel and leaving her in the dark hallway where a thin column of flickering light reflected on the wall adjacent to the door. She stared at it for a few moments, wondering what to make of her host who had seemed to have not a care in the world until his cryptic comment.

That she felt drawn to Mr. Debenham she ascribed to her exhaustion and to his having saved her from an undesirable fate. Now was no time to give in to silly romantic feelings—John needed her. Her father needed her.

CHAPTER 4

$\mathcal{T}$he next morning, Lawrence took long strides down the hall, his boots making a muffled but rhythmic noise as they hit the long, maroon rug lining the floor. His stomach growled, and his jaw tightened as he thought on the letter he had received. The steward his father had hired had conveyed in no uncertain terms that the estate demanded his immediate attention. He wanted to meet in person.

If Lawrence wouldn't let his parents bully him into putting the estate in order, he certainly wouldn't let a stranger do so, steward or no. The fact that his father hadn't been able to let go of the reins enough to allow Lawrence himself the hiring of a steward was further evidence of his insistence on having control over all aspects of Lawrence's life.

He could only guess that his father was corresponding with the man, checking up on Lawrence and his progress. The whole gifting of the estate smelled strongly of a test. And Lawrence was not willing to be tested. He took in an irritated breath.

As he approached the drawing room, he heard the sound of laughter float through the door which had been left ajar. One of those laughs was easily identified as belonging to Mr. Adley—loud and guttural. The other laugh was softer and decidedly feminine—surely the laugh of Miss Renwick.

Lawrence's lips pursed. He had assumed that Miss Renwick would stay abed later—he definitely hadn't intended for her to encounter Mr. Adley and Mr. Bower without him there to perform an introduction—and to perhaps prepare her for what to expect from them.

He supposed he should have known Miss Renwick wasn't the type to keep late morning hours, though. She seemed more like his mother—awake with the rising sun, having accomplished most of her necessary tasks before breakfast. He sighed. Hopefully Miss Renwick was none the worse for her encounter with his friends.

"We are talking of the same Mr. Lawrence Debenham, are we not?" Adley's voice drifted into the hallway, full of incredulity.

Lawrence slowed his gait, coming to a halt just shy of the door. What was Adley about?

"Yes," Miss Renwick's voice said slowly. "That is, I assume so. I know only one gentleman by that name, but he is certainly the one who brought us here last night."

"Come now, Adley," Bower said in his halting speech.

The corner of Lawrence's mouth lifted in a smile. Bower was not a man of many words, nor was he particularly skilled in speaking those few words, but Lawrence always paid close attention when the man spoke. There was often a streak of wisdom in his words that most people wrote off due to their poor delivery.

"Stands to reason," Bower continued, "she couldn't be here talking with us in Deb's drawing room if it wasn't Deb she met last night."

"Hmph," said Adley, clearly considering his friend's words. "Well, stap me! Never knew Deb to be a dashed knight in shining armor before."

Lawrence thought it was time to step in. He opened the door, clearing his throat as he entered. His gaze flitted to Miss Renwick, curious for her response to Adley's ridiculous words about knights in shining armor. There seemed to be a slight pink tinge to her cheeks, but she offered him a smile and a slight nod free of any reserve when their eyes met. With the full morning light coming through the room's two windows, it was Lawrence's first time seeing her in daylight.

Gad, but she was prettier than he'd remembered.

"Ah, Deb!" Adley said. "Wondered when we'd see you. We've just made Miss Renwick's acquaintance." He left the last word with an upward inflection, directing a significant glance at Lawrence as if to question why he even had such an opportunity.

Lawrence pointedly avoided his gaze. "Ah, yes, my apologies, Miss Renwick." He shot her a teasing smile. "I would never have left you to these fellows alone if I had known." He looked around the room and then back to Miss Renwick. "Is John still abed, then?"

"John?" Mr. Adley said, pausing with his glass of ale mid-air. "Dash it, Deb! Should've told us if you planned to invite the entire county."

Bower shook his head rapidly with a finger wagging in the air as he finished swallowing a bite of his toast. "Couldn't possibly invite the county. Deb's not such a slow-top. He's only got six beds."

Adley looked at Bower for a moment, his mouth hanging open as if he were deciding whether or not to reply. He seemed to decide against it, though, and turned back toward Lawrence. "Then who's this John fellow keeping London hours in the country?"

"John is my youngest brother," Miss Renwick explained. "We were traveling together when the carriage wheel broke."

Lawrence could hear the apology in her voice. It had been apparent from his very first offer of aid that she felt no small degree of guilt for imposing upon him. And Mr. Adley's thoughtless comments were clearly doing nothing to alleviate that.

"She already said that, Adley," Bower pointed out. "Must listen when a lady talks, you know."

Lawrence's mouth twitched, and Adley looked stunned.

He turned his head to Miss Renwick. "My apologies, ma'am," he said in a chastised voice. "I have apparently been remiss in my attentions."

"Not at all," she said. "I have been informed on more than one occasion by my younger brother Richard that one cannot be expected to retain any information before noon."

Mr. Adley looked very much struck at her comment, his head nodding slowly and then gaining speed. "I think I should like this brother of yours. Wise beyond his years, I should say!"

Lawrence smiled, gratified to see that Miss Renwick and his friends seemed to be getting on well, and took his seat at the head of the table. He filled his cup with ale and began buttering his toast when the door opened once again.

John appeared, his shirt rumpled, both fists rubbing at his eyes. The door opened wider, and Anne slid past John, heading straight for Adley.

Adley yelled out and recoiled, nearly tipping over in his chair to avoid the mass of dark fur accosting him. Miss Renwick shot up from her seat, embarrassment and apology on her face as she called to Anne in a stern voice.

Unperturbed by her less-than-warm reception, Anne trotted over to Miss Renwick, sitting obediently at her side and panting, her eyes barely visible beneath the clumps of fur hanging from her head.

"Good gracious," Adley called out, staring at the dog with misgiving as he leaned away with his knife raised tentatively. "What is it?"

John ran over to Anne's side, crying out in a voice of deep offense, "She's not an 'it!' She's Anne!" He put a loving hand on the dog's face. "Don't mind him, Anne."

Mr. Adley didn't lower his knife an inch, and his expression was more confused than ever. "Eh?"

Lawrence's shoulders shook as he looked on, leaning back in his seat, content to observe the fiasco taking place in his drawing room.

"Dog," said Bower between bites of a roll with preserves slathered generously on it. "Plain as a pikestaff."

"She is a dog," Miss Renwick confirmed apologetically. "One without any manners to speak of." She looked censoriously at Anne who panted contentedly as John stroked her fur.

"Anne, you say?" Mr. Adley said.

John glanced at Mr. Adley through suspicious, narrowed eyes and then nodded.

"Yes, Anne," said Lawrence in a falsely impatient voice. "What else should she be named? Come, Adley. Use your head. Anne as in Anne Bonny the pirate."

Mr. Adley turned to look at Lawrence, his brows raised.

Lawrence stifled his smile and nodded. When he had offered his home to the Renwicks, he hadn't considered what Mr. Adley and Mr. Bower would make of the guests. The result so far was more entertaining than he could have imagined.

Miss Renwick pulled out a chair on her other side, indicating that John should seat himself there, and began making her brother a plate of food.

John looked on with hungry eyes as his sister buttered a roll, going so far as to lick his lips as she spread the preserves. Miss Renwick's food sat waiting on her plate, and suddenly Lawrence found himself wondering whether he should have offered to make John's plate of food instead.

John munched happily on his food, slipping a few bits to Anne when he thought no one was watching. When he finally realized that Lawrence was observing him, he shrank slightly, pulling his hand away from Anne's mouth and looking terrified that Lawrence might inform his sister on him. Lawrence winked, and John smiled back, relaxing.

"Lawrie?" John said, causing Adley to turn in his seat and stare. Lawrence had always insisted that his friends refer to him as simply "Deb." It was hardly a secret that he despised both his first name—a name he shared with his father—and the nickname used to differentiate between the two of them amongst their family: Lawrie.

Lawrence avoided his friend's eyes, but it was too late. Bower was leaning across the table toward John.

"Best not to call him that," he said in an attempted whisper. Bower had never been able to speak softly, though. "Devilish particular about his name, he is."

Miss Renwick's gaze rested on Lawrence, watching his reaction. Lawrence forced a smile, shaking his head to rebut Bower's words while trying to catch his eye.

John glared at Bower. "He gave me special permission on account of I can't say Debren—Deneb—" he huffed in frustration "—his name."

"Not to worry," said Mr. Adley, seeing Lawrence's warning look. "Deb might plant me a facer for calling him that, but he won't do it to you."

John's eyes narrowed, and his fists came up. "I shouldn't let him even if he tried! Charlie Simms taught me how to draw a man's cork."

Miss Renwick's eyes widened, and she put her hand over John's fists, pushing them back down into his lap and saying in a determinedly bright tone, "What shall we do today, John?"

John sat up straight in his chair, looking at his sister with excitement in his round eyes. "I saw a big stream from the window, and it even has a bridge!"

Miss Renwick nodded with feigned interest, sipping her tea.

"May we go there after breakfast?" John asked in pleading tones.

Miss Renwick set down the teacup. "I think you should perhaps ask Mr. Debenham, as it is his estate."

John turned toward Lawrence, his bright eyes staring into Lawrence's as if his every last hope depended on the answer. "Will you come play at the stream with us, Lawrie?"

Miss Renwick laughed, but her eyes flew to Lawrence's. "That is not quite what I meant, John. I only meant that we should ask his permission to visit the stream as we are his guests. I'm sure Mr. Debenham has plenty to occupy him having just moved into this house."

Lawrence shifted in his seat, and Mr. Adley slapped his thigh with a large laugh. "Just moved in? Bless you, he's been here going on two months."

Miss Renwick's confusion was simultaneously endearing and uncomfortable. Lawrence couldn't blame her for the assumption—not when he had only two servants and a house still largely shrouded in dust and holland covers. If she and John ventured out of doors, they would see firsthand the wild forces of nature at work in the gardens, the unkempt lawns, and the general state of disrepair.

Since leaving the family estate in Surrey and arriving at Holywell House, Lawrence had taken a morbid satisfaction in viewing the disrepair all around him—when he had thought about it at all. Most of the time, he was too busy enjoying himself to notice.

The simple knowledge that he was defying his parents' expectations had made him feel master of something for once. The physical distance between him and his father finally matched the emotional distance he had felt for years, and it gave him the freedom to make his own decisions without his father's zealous gaze ensuring exact obedience. He could finally relax and enjoy life, something he had been taking full advantage of—with the help of Mr. Adley and Mr. Bower.

But the satisfaction Lawrence had felt in leaving the house to deteriorate suddenly made his cravat feel tight. He felt petty and juvenile; embarrassed of this estate that Miss Renwick had assumed to be only recently inhabited based on its neglected condition.

Miss Renwick cleared her throat quietly and said, "Well, whatever the case, I am sure he has much better things to do."

"Do you have better things to do than coming with us?" John said, directing his sincere gaze at Lawrence who was still trying to decide what to do with the feelings brought up by Miss Renwick's assumption.

Lawrence's half-smile appeared as he looked at John. How could anyone resist such a hopeful gaze?

In truth, he had nothing on his schedule. His days were generally made up of card-playing, hunting, and the odd trip out to watch a cock-fight or a boxing match. An hour spent with the Renwicks might just be the refreshing change he needed from a life that had begun to feel a bit monotonous. Besides, John had long since put to rest any worry Lawrence might have of being bored in his company.

And Miss Renwick...well, she was a bit of an enigma. She was clearly a capable young woman, accustomed to having charge of her younger brother, though she couldn't have been out more than three years herself. And though she often spoke to John with sternness, Lawrence hadn't missed the glint of humor in her eye when John had done or said something unpredictable. She was much more skilled at suppressing a smile than Lawrence was.

"How could I possibly have anything better to do?" Lawrence said, setting down his cup decidedly. "I would be honored to show you my humble stream."

John rubbed his hands together in delight, and Miss Renwick shot Lawrence a warm smile that put paid to his decision to accompany them.

"We shall just go change, then," she said, glancing at the clock on the mantelpiece. "We can be ready by—" Her brows knitted together.

"Doesn't work," Bower said. "Hasn't been wound."

Miss Renwick nodded her comprehension, but her glance flitted back to the clock as she hurried John out of the room, leaving Lawrence with his friends.

Through the corner of his eye, Lawrence was aware that Mr. Adley was staring at him with one eyebrow raised.

"Show them your humble stream, eh?" Adley said. "That's if you can even find it!" He shook his head in a deeply disapproving gesture. "Shouldn't be at all surprised if I know these grounds better than you."

"Don't be ridiculous, Adley," Lawrence said. He knew just where the stream was. He'd seen it any number of times. That it would be his first time seeing it from a vantage point other than his dressing room window was beside the point.

"Not ridiculous, Deb," interjected Bower. "Heard you consign this place to the devil time and again. Just yesterday you said—"

"Thank you, Bower," Lawrence interrupted, pushing his chair back to stand. "I know what I've said. What that has to say to things, though, I'm sure I don't know! The boy wants to see the stream, so I'll show him the stream." He made an irritated gesture with his hand.

Mr. Adley scoffed. "Don't know what's come over you, Deb." He shook his head rapidly. "Hardly recognize you—rescuing damsels in distress, inviting guests at the drop of a hat, allowing strange beasts at the breakfast table, playing nurse maid to a lad barely breeched? Something havey-cavey about it all. I don't like it." He looked at Lawrence with a significant tilt to his eyebrows.

"You aren't required to like it, Adley."

Mr. Adley nodded slowly and shifted his gaze to his plate. He grabbed his cup, pausing just before he took a drink to say with studied nonchalance, "She's devilish handsome." His eyes flitted to Lawrence for a brief moment as he sipped his drink.

Mr. Bower was buttering his fourth roll, but he nodded his head firmly. "A very fine-looking dog. Anne, wasn't it?"

Mr. Adley slapped his hand on the table. "Not the dog, Bower. Miss Renwick!"

Bower's head came up, and he looked at Mr. Adley, comprehension slowly dawning in his eyes. "Ah, my mistake." He looked at Lawrence. "Sorry, Deb. Didn't mean to give offense. Misunderstood. That's all."

Lawrence scoffed loudly. "You say you hardly recognize me? You are the ones being ridiculous."

He stalked out of the room, his jaw set tightly. Mr. Adley's words had irritated him, but only because they had struck a chord. Lawrence hardly recognized himself in this whole situation. But he couldn't well leave a young woman and a child in a carriage yard at night, could he? He would have to be cold-blooded to leave them there with no place to stay. There was nothing havey-cavey about it.

And as for Miss Renwick being handsome—what had that to say

to anything? Surely Adley and Bower knew him well enough to know that Lawrence had no idea of marriage, no matter how handsome a woman might be. Now that he was finally out from under his parents' thumb, he couldn't—he wouldn't—let a woman trap him into a marriage where he would spend the rest of his life under a new thumb, as beautiful as Miss Renwick might be.

He couldn't imagine that Miss Renwick would be as dictatorial as his parents, but that was beside the point. Marriage was not something Lawrence was considering.

There was no need for dramatics from Adley and Bower. The Renwicks would leave in two days, and then Lawrence's life would go back to the way it was before.

CHAPTER 5

*E*leanor stood in the entry hall with John. She smoothed the fabric of her white walking dress and brushed a spot of dust from the sleeve of her cornflower blue spencer. For some reason, she felt keenly aware of the absence of her maid. Jane had such a way with her hair, always achieving results that Eleanor herself couldn't.

She had been sure that she was acting with great presence of mind in sending Jane ahead with their belongings to set everything in order for their arrival, but the decision seemed foolish now. Dangerous, even.

What if she and John had been accosted on the road by highwaymen? Their coachman carried a blunderbuss, to be sure, but having two servants instead of one could prove the difference between safety and injury in such situations. Not that Jane could be considered an asset in any situation requiring even the smallest bit of courage. She was notoriously quick to become weak in the knees and couldn't bear the sight of blood.

Eleanor tucked a curl under her bonnet. At least the bonnet would hide her hair while they were outside. And her curls should keep well enough until the carriage wheel was repaired—tomorrow, if the man was to be believed. Why she felt such a concern for her appearance was a fact she didn't care to examine more closely. She had a sneaking suspicion that it had some connection to Mr. Debenham, and such a ridiculous idea was better ignored than inspected.

She looked to John who was staring up at the tall ceiling with his mouth agape. Anne laid on the cool stone floor beside him. Eleanor followed his gaze and blinked when she saw the sheet of cobwebs above. Mr. Adley had insisted that Mr. Debenham had been living here for some time.

She couldn't understand why he would choose to live in such a state. She had considered that perhaps it was a matter of lacking the resources to set it aright, but his dress, the elegant carriage they had traveled in, and the well-stocked breakfast table belied that assumption. Why, then, would he choose to only have two servants? They must be worked to the bone in an estate the size of Holywell House.

"I apologize." The voice of Mr. Debenham echoed in the hall as he walked through the archway that led in from the main hallway.

Eleanor brought her head down to meet his eyes, smiling amid an uncomfortable swallow. To think he should have seen her passing judgment on his home when he had so kindly opened it up to them brought heat to her cheeks.

John seemed to forget the presence of the massive blanket of cobwebs above, shouting, "You came!"

Mr. Debenham smiled in amusement. "Of course I did! Let's be on our way, shall we?"

John nodded enthusiastically, and Mr. Debenham opened the front door, watching as John skipped outside with Anne on his heels. Eleanor thanked him as she passed through, and he nodded with a smile.

It was a grey day, and clouds blanketed the sky much as the cobwebs had done to the entry hall ceiling. In the diffused light of day, Eleanor had the opportunity to take in the surroundings which had been shrouded in darkness the night before.

The house itself was stately—or should have been, had it been stripped of the thick façade of ivy covering the cream-colored stone underneath. As it stood, the ivy had crept around the windows, intruding on the light that otherwise would have shone through. The pebbled courtyard was punctuated with weeds which poked through and towered over the rocks beneath.

The four of them traipsed toward a copse of trees which stood on the other side of a field, John marching ahead, creating a path of some sort through the tall green alfalfa. He suddenly cried out in exulting accents, stooping down, and emerging with a large stick. He held it out like a sword toward Mr. Debenham. "*En guarde!*"

Mr. Debenham held up his hands in surrender. "I never agree to an uneven fight!"

He kept his hands up as his eyes searched among the alfalfa. He shot a hand down and brought out a stick of his own, much shorter than John's. John's face lit up with excitement, and Eleanor looked on with an indulgent smile.

"Perhaps," she said, giving a wide berth to the two who had assumed a fencing stance, "we might delay this match until we reach the stream?"

The two of them exchanged glances and then dropped their arms to their sides. John marched on ahead, using his stick to beat away all the offending alfalfa blocking their path.

"If he is already going to the work of whacking at all this over-growth," Mr. Debenham said, observing John with a half-smile, "I should at least arm him with a scythe."

Eleanor's eyes widened at the image of John wielding such a tool. "For the love of all you hold dear," she said, "please don't even consider such a thing. John is much more skilled in his imagination than he is in body. We should all be in grave danger if he were to wield such an object."

As if to confirm Eleanor's words, Anne gave a small yelp as the butt of John's stick came in contact with one of her legs. John apologized to the dog but continued whacking at the grass with just as much zeal as before.

Mr. Debenham tossed his head back in a hearty laugh, and Eleanor covered her mouth with a hand as she tried—unsuccessfully —to stifle her own sense of the ridiculous. The task of being with John day and night had been wearing on her, and she had found herself feeling impatient or frustrated with many of his antics. But somehow those same antics elicited a desire to laugh now that she had someone else to observe them with.

A glance at Mr. Debenham confirmed to her that he was at his most handsome when the corners of his eyes wrinkled in laughter. She hurriedly looked away. It was perhaps better not to look at him while he was laughing.

She cleared her throat. "Mr. Adley and Mr. Bower were very kind. Are they relatives or simply friends of yours?"

Mr. Debenham's eyes stayed on John, his mouth stretched in a smile. "They are only friends, but I consider them to be my family." His smile faltered a bit.

Eleanor nodded her understanding. "At times I have thought that it would be nice to be able to choose one's family." She had wished for a sister on more than one occasion.

Mr. Debenham's brows were knitted together, a stark contrast from his smile only moments before. "I have had the same thought on more occasions than I can count."

Eleanor smiled, chancing an upward glance at him. "Wishing for a brother like John, no doubt? One who constantly plagues you to play pirates with him?"

The side of Mr. Debenham's mouth quirked up briefly, and Eleanor felt a satisfaction in having lightened his frown. "I would have loved a younger brother like John growing up. As it was, I was sent to separate schools from my brothers. And my visits home never permitted for entertainment with them. My father was very particular about how I spent my time."

Eleanor turned her head to look at him beside her. The playful banter she had begun to expect from him was extinguished as he spoke of his family, his eyes harsher than she had seen them.

"One's parents have such a say in the quality of one's life, don't they?" she said, grimacing in understanding as he looked at her. She watched as John raced Anne. "My childhood was idyllic in many ways—my parents both loving and indulgent. It wasn't until my mother's death and my father's all-consuming grief that I understood how much of my happiness and sense of security had relied on them."

The corners of Mr. Debenham's mouth were turned down in a thoughtful frown. "Has your father recovered from his grief?"

Eleanor shook her head, trying to smile to counter the frustration she felt. "I still have hope that he will, though."

A silence, strangely comfortable, reigned between them for the last minute of their walk. When they arrived at the stream, Eleanor took in a contented breath. As unkempt as the area was, there was a rugged beauty in the overgrown state of everything.

Cornflowers lined the edges of the stream and encircled the bases of the thick trees. Downstream a small, wooden bridge spanned the length of the gurgling stream, and the sound of birds chirping up above added to the musical sound of trickling water.

"There's the bridge!" John cried, running toward it.

Eleanor and Mr. Debenham followed behind Anne whose nose seemed torn between the multitude of scents to be found in the air and on the ground.

The bridge was dilapidated, with a large pocket in the middle where the wood had given way completely. John ran toward it, leaping in excitement.

"John," cried out Eleanor, and he came to a halt. She indicated the middle of the bridge with a finger. "It's not safe, love."

"Phooey!" cried John. "I can walk on the sides just fine."

Eleanor bit her lip.

Mr. Debenham approached the bridge, scanning it and prodding at parts with the stick he held. A long board rested in the grass beside the stream, and he picked it up, inspecting it for a moment before he laid it across the bridge so that it stretched the width of the stream.

He turned around suddenly, scrunching his shoulders and

holding out his stick toward John with one eye squinted. "Arr! So ye wish to walk the plank, do ye?"

John smiled and lifted his chin, shooting a quick glance at Eleanor before setting one foot on the board.

Eleanor opened her mouth to remonstrate but instead bit her lip as she watched John balance across. It wasn't dangerous precisely. While the middle section of the bridge was missing, the rest of the structure was intact, providing side boards for footing if Mr. Debenham's plank happened to buckle.

Once John arrived at the other side, he raised his stick in the air triumphantly, and Eleanor couldn't help but smile.

"Aye!" cried Mr. Debenham in a hoarse voice, as he walked the plank deftly, stopping once he reached the end. "Ye've walked the plank successfully, but now the lady must walk it!" He whipped around toward Eleanor, his expression a mixture between menacing and laughing.

John dropped his sword with a scoffing sound. "Nell never plays pirates! And she's sure to fall in if she tries to walk across."

Eleanor raised her brows, her pride piqued. It was true that she didn't play pirates. She had always felt that it was more important for her to set the example of decorum and responsibility to a brother whose imagination often ran wild. But for John to say such a thing in front of Mr. Debenham, besides insinuating that she was inelegant enough to make falling into the stream a foregone conclusion...well, it was unjust.

"Oh ho!" she said, grabbing a crooked stick from the weeds at her feet. "I shall fall in, shall I?" She tapped the stick on the bridge and sent a challenging look to John and Mr. Debenham.

John's jaw hung loose as he stared at Eleanor with wide eyes. Mr. Debenham looked intrigued. He kept his position at the far end of the bridge and made a grand welcoming gesture with his hand, inviting her to step toward him.

Eleanor smiled and took in a breath before stepping onto the bridge. She glanced down through the gap between the board she was walking on and the sides of the bridge. She wasn't afraid of drowning—the stream wasn't more than a foot deep—but the prospect of falling in and making a fool of herself still made her anxious. She regretted picking up the stick as it made her feel unevenly weighted and deprived of the use of one hand should she lose her balance.

She set one foot in front of the other, watching her half boot appear from under her skirts. The board wobbled, and she teetered for a moment.

"Don't look down," Mr. Debenham said, his pirate voice gone.

She looked up at him, and though he smiled at her, his eyes watched her without wavering.

"If you watch what you're doing too carefully, you'll fall. Try not to overthink it. Just keep your eyes on me."

She swallowed, thinking that she was much more likely to fall by keeping her eyes on the handsome face which was getting closer and closer with each step. But it would be rude to disregard his counsel, so she obeyed, keeping her eyes trained on his which, she noted, were an almost perfect match to the color of the bridge. His smile grew as she neared him, and he put out a hand to receive her.

Feeling a small sense of exhilaration now that she was almost across, Eleanor extended her stick past Mr. Debenham's hand and paused, looking at John and saying, "You have grossly underestimated me, John."

The board wobbled underneath her, and she tottered, dropping her stick as she tried to regain her balance. She stumbled forward where Mr. Debenham's hand shot out to catch her arm.

He stabilized her, gripping both of her arms.

Eleanor looked up from the flowing water below, meeting eyes with him. His eyes didn't match the color of the bridge wood at all. They were far too warm a shade of brown. And they had a deep green rim.

"Ha!" called out John. "I told you she would fall, didn't I, Lawrie?"

Mr. Debenham's eyes danced, and Eleanor revised her opinion.

He was not at his most engaging when laughing but rather when he was trying not to laugh.

Anne barked, jarring Eleanor from her troublesome thoughts and reminding them all with a whine that she was the only one left on the other side of the bridge.

Mr. Debenham released his stabilizing grip on her arms, and Eleanor ignored how her arms seemed to tingle where his hands had been.

John called to Anne, and she ran up to the beam, hesitating and then running across deftly.

"You see, Nell?" John said, petting the dog with pride. "Anne's a girl, and she didn't fall."

Anne barked and ran to the water's edge where she drank freely from the stream. John followed her, prodding at a large rock with his stick. He eyed the shoreline and picked up a smaller stick, throwing it into the stream where Anne pounced after it, emerging with fur sopping wet from her belly down to her paws. The picture she presented—voluminous, puffy fur on top, matted fur which clung to her legs on bottom—made them all laugh.

Anne stepped onto the shore, dropped the prized stick onto the grass, and began shaking her fur. Eleanor cried out and drew both hands in front her face to stop the spray of stream water which wetted her cheeks and clothing.

John giggled and then used his stick to splash the dog with water as retribution. Anne looked at him for a moment, completely still.

"Oh no," Mr. Debenham said slowly. Eleanor felt his hand grab hers and pull her away right as Anne began a second shaking.

Eleanor cried out again, letting Mr. Debenham pull her to safety as she laughed and put a hand up to steady her bonnet. Seeming to think it was all a game, John joined in with Anne, splashing the water towards them with the stick as he called out like a pirate.

Eleanor and Mr. Debenham slowed as they reached the limit of John's range. Mr. Debenham's hand lingered in hers as they looked back toward John, laughing and slightly breathless.

He turned toward Eleanor, a large grin spread across his face. It flickered slightly as their eyes met and his gaze flitted toward their hands. He let her hand drop, glancing at her and then toward John whose face was covered in water droplets, his hair tossed in a state of mixed wet and dry.

Eleanor stole a glance at Mr. Debenham, noting with a swallow the way his jaw had tightened and his smile had a forced quality to it.

"John," she said, "I think we should be getting back." She looked at his pants which had become spattered with mud amongst all the water. " You'll need a change of clothes, I'm afraid."

She put a hand up to feel her hair. One of her curls had fallen victim to John's splashing antics. She sighed. It didn't matter, really. They had very little time left with Mr. Debenham. Nor could she forget the way he had looked so serious after letting go of her hand. It had clearly been a mistake.

CHAPTER 6

*L*awrence strode through the grass just in front of Eleanor, John, and the dog. He had suggested a different route home —taking the road—since the wet state of their clothing made them likely to attract no small amount of dirt in a walk through the alfalfa field.

He clenched his hand. He had grabbed Miss Renwick's hand in a thoughtless moment, hoping to spare her from becoming soaked by the dog. But somehow he had kept his hand in hers even after it was necessary, and for some reason, he couldn't stop thinking about how it had felt. He had felt immediate embarrassment for the presumption, innocent as it had been, but Miss Renwick hadn't seemed bothered by it.

Seeing her take up the implicit challenge issued by John to cross the stream, watching her laugh in the midst of being sprayed—it had been completely unexpected from someone who seemed to take life very seriously. Lawrence had caught a glimpse of Miss Renwick's genuine laugh—one that she tried to hide by putting a hand in front of her mouth. But that hand couldn't mask the enjoyment twinkling in her eyes.

Lawrence cleared his throat, stepping onto the dirt lane that led to Holywell House. Thinking such things of Miss Renwick was counterproductive. If there was one thing his parents wanted as much as to see him running the estate to perfection, it was for him to settle down and marry. To do either would be to surrender to two people who were always used to having their way, who had come to take for granted that their son would do whatever they wanted—and in the precise way they wanted.

John ran up beside Lawrence, looking up at him with hesitant eyes. "Lawrie, are you angry at me?"

Lawrence's shoulders dropped, and he chuckled. "Of course not." He mussed John's hair as evidence of his words.

John's lower lip jutted out. "You looked very angry. That is always how Papa looks when he is unhappy with me."

Lawrence shot a look at Miss Renwick whose hands were clasped behind her back, her eyes directed at the ground in front of her. Had she also assumed he was angry?

"No, my good man," he said to John. "In fact...." He snatched at one of the long, butter-colored stalks lining their path and thrust it out toward John. "*En guarde!*"

John snatched one of his own, parrying an attempted thrust by Lawrence, but both of their stalks bent, the chaff weighing them down.

"Hmm," Lawrence said, inspecting his makeshift sword. "I find my sword somewhat lacking."

The sound of horse hooves and turning wheels brought them all around. A one-horse wagon, driven by a man in farming garb approached them. In the wagon sat three small children. Two held apples in their hands, while the third and youngest seemed determined to have a bite of one of her siblings' apples.

Lawrence turned back away from the wagon and continued walking on the edge of the road to let the wagon pass. He hadn't interacted with any of his tenants in person, so he expected nothing but a friendly nod.

The wagon wheels slowed, and Lawrence heard the children calling out, "Dog! Dog!" He turned around. The Renwicks had both stopped walking to let the wagon pass, and Miss Renwick was looking at the group in the wagon with a friendly smile.

The children jumped out of the wagon, the youngest trailing behind, and skipped over to the dog who greeted them with a tail wagging frantically. The man who Lawrence assumed to be their father watched them with a large grin on his sun-tanned, wrinkled face. His eyes flitted over to Lawrence, though, and the smile wavered slightly.

Accepting that he could no longer avoid the interaction, Lawrence nodded, and the man returned the nod, tipping his wide-brimmed hat.

"Mr. Debenham, I presume?" the farmer said, coming down from the seat of the wagon. "My name is Joseph Foster. I live just at the end of this bend." He indicated the road behind him with his head.

"Right next to the river?" John said, awe-struck.

Farmer Foster nodded.

The envy in John's eyes made Lawrence bite his lip.

"You must play in the river every day!" John said in near reverence. "I know I would if I lived so close. We never had any rivers by us in London—well, 'cept the Thames, but I only swam in there once, and Nell knew right away on account of I smelled bad."

Lawrence stifled a laugh and caught eyes with Miss Renwick who nodded to confirm the story, a hint of that alluring twinkle in her eyes. He could only imagine all the stories she had with a younger brother like John in her charge.

"We swim after we work in the fields in the summer," piped in one of the girls as she tried to swipe at Anne's swooshing tail.

Farmer Foster looked at Lawrence, slight hesitation written on his brow. "Speaking of working the fields, sir," he said, "the village is ready and willing to harvest these fields for you." He looked out over the alfalfa fields. "They're in prime state for harvesting, and we'd all be glad for the work."

Lawrence's brow furrowed as he looked toward the fields. He hadn't even considered that the field would need harvesting or that it would fall to him to arrange. He smiled. "That's kind of you, but I don't think I shall harvest this year."

Harvesting was likely one of the things his father expected him to undertake—no doubt there was a very particular way he would believe it should be done. Lawrence's jaw tightened. He had no intention of folding under pressure—at least not until he had shown his parents that he was his own master and had no intention of bowing to the obligation they made him feel.

Farmer Foster's jaw hung slack, and Lawrence could see Miss Renwick looking at him, blinking slowly.

"No plans to harvest?" Farmer Foster said, incredulous.

Lawrence straightened his shoulders a bit, feeling uncomfortable with their gazes on him.

"But sir," Farmer Foster said, his voice betraying his desperation, "our village won't survive the winter."

Lawrence bit the inside of his lip, avoiding Miss Renwick's eyes. He hadn't wanted Holywell House. He had done his level best to explain that to his father when he had informed him of the purchase and plans. His father had only become angry, accusing Lawrence of ingratitude and threatening to rein in his allowance. So Lawrence had come.

But the sense of freedom he had felt upon his arrival at Holywell House had overcome him, and anytime the creeping feeling of the obligations he was neglecting came upon him, he shoved them to the back of his mind, opting for more of the lighthearted entertainment which Adley and Bower were so anxious to show him.

The result was that all considerations more serious than who should win the next boxing match in town were driven from his mind. He hadn't paused to contemplate that there might be sufferers apart from his parents if he left the estate in disrepair.

For the second time in a day, he felt petty and foolish for his intentional negligence. And he didn't relish the feeling. Somehow it felt connected to Miss Renwick—before she had come, he had been getting along just fine, unplagued by such uncomfortable notions of himself.

"What did you say your name was?" he asked the farmer, feeling the need to fill the silence.

"Joseph Foster, sir," the man said, doffing his hat and holding it against his chest in both hands. "Perhaps you've seen the letters I've sent? Two since your arrival in June." He dropped the hat to his side, his posture becoming more confident. "I acted as bailiff for Mr. Compton—the gentleman who lived at Holywell House before."

Lawrence thought he recollected his housekeeper handing him a stack of letters once, but he had been on his way out the door and had no memory of where he had put them. He didn't know anyone in the vicinity, after all, so he had assumed they couldn't have been of great import.

"Hmm. I must have missed the letters," Lawrence said. "I have been somewhat occupied since my arrival, but I shall ask if any of the servants are aware of them." It was true that he had been occupied since arriving, but the activities he had been occupied with had been unrelated to estate matters.

Farmer Foster nodded, and the look of hesitation crossed his face again. "I don't wish to overwhelm you, sir, but I know that there are some matters in the village in need of attention. Mr. Compton left without much notice, and the village has been without means of repairs since his departure. If you have but five minutes, I could show you...." He trailed off, pointing in the direction of the village.

Lawrence felt his muscles clenching. It wasn't that he was opposed to helping the villagers, though he would be lying if he said he had considered them much before now. It was simply that he had become used to digging in his heels whenever he felt more obligation being thrust upon him.

Farmer Foster seemed a nice enough man, but what he was asking was precisely the sort of thing Lawrence's father had hoped to accomplish in sending him to Holywell House. If Lawrence began arranging for repairs and harvests and such, he was as good as complying with his father's will.

He glanced at Miss Renwick who smiled and nodded. "We would be happy to join with you if you are agreeable. I have a feeling that I will be called upon to manage much of my father's new estate, so anything I can learn by observing—" she looked at Farmer Foster "—would be wonderful."

Feeling stuck between a rock and hard place, Lawrence nodded his assent.

Farmer Foster called for his children to hop back into the wagon but ended in assenting to their following along with the dog to whom they seemed to have taken a great liking. Lawrence walked beside Farmer Foster, inviting Miss Renwick to join them in their conversation. She sent him a warm look of gratitude at the offer, and Lawrence felt a bit of his irritation slip away.

They passed by the tenant homes in the village, and Lawrence had the impression that his cravat was tightening with each one they passed. It was evident that the village was in a state as bad as Holywell House. The thatching on the roofs was almost nonexistent in some places.

Farmer Foster followed Lawrence's gaze, setting a loving hand on the head of his son who had come up beside him. "Every bird nest within ten miles must have come from the village roofs, I reckon."

Lawrence was mostly quiet, feeling pensive and conflicted by what he was seeing. Miss Renwick, on the other hand, seemed full of questions, though she looked at Lawrence tentatively before asking them. He gave a low chuckle and then his permission to ask whatever pleased her. The questions she asked were intelligent, practical ones, and Farmer Foster seemed always to have an answer.

When she commented that it was hard to believe what quick work the birds had made of the thatching, Farmer Foster admitted that the state of the roofs reflected two years of it.

"The thatching wasn't replenished last year, then?" Miss Renwick said. Lawrence noted how engaged she was in her conversation with the farmer. She held her hands clasped in front of her and her brow furrowed as she listened to his response.

"Without wishing to speak ill of Mr. Compton," Farmer Foster said, "he kept his purse strings very tight. I did my best to help him understand that the success of his estate and his purse depended upon the happiness of his tenants, but he could never be persuaded to see it that way."

Lawrence cleared his throat, feeling supremely uncomfortable as his conscience nagged at him. Surely the villagers had hoped that their new landlord would be more committed to their common interests. Instead they had him.

They arrived at the end of the lane, and Miss Renwick looked up to the last house. "And this is your home, Mr. Foster?"

He nodded, looking through one of the dirty windows to a woman who was about her tasks. "It's where the heart is."

Lawrence looked at the roof. Its condition was by far the worst of any of the homes.

"Your roof needs immediate attention," Miss Renwick said, pointing at a particularly large spot near the chimney where no thatching was visible.

The oldest Foster daughter followed Miss Renwick's finger and said practically, "Papa gave his money to the Palmers to fix their wagon, but he says that after the fall wheat harvest, he can fill the holes in time for the first frost."

Farmer Foster's son tugged on his father's shirt, looking up at him with large, brown eyes. "Is that man going to fix the leaks in our roof, Papa?" He shot a timid glance at Lawrence who shifted his weight.

The youngest girl who had both arms around Anne looked up. "And our chimney, too? I can't sleep when Mama coughs at night."

Farmer Foster looked as uncomfortable as Lawrence felt. Lawrence stepped toward the dog, kneeling down and petting her as he looked at the little girl. "I shall send someone over tomorrow."

Farmer Foster took in a breath and smiled before looking down at his daughter. "All right, your mother needs help inside. Get your siblings and help her out with dinner."

When he bid Lawrence and the Renwicks goodbye shortly after, a hint of embarrassment and discomfort was still apparent in his demeanor.

Lawrence walked in silence as they traveled back down the dirty road toward Holywell House. The Fosters had given him much to think on—much to reconsider. Before now, the cost of disregarding his parents' wishes and expectations had seemed to be well worth his defiance. It was apparent, though, that the actual cost was much greater than he thought—and greatest by far to the tenants.

"I like the Fosters," John said, skipping to catch up with his sister and Lawrence. "Can I help them with the harvesting?"

Miss Renwick laughed. "Because you wish to swim in the stream with them afterward?"

John nodded, unabashed. "Alice Foster said that there is a little whirlpool downstream with water much deeper than the bridge has."

Miss Renwick put a hand on his shoulder. "I don't think we shall be here for the harvest, love. The carriage should be fixed by tomorrow, I hope."

John let out a large, discontented sigh, his shoulders stooping. "I don't want to go. I like it here with Lawrie."

"Yes, he has been very good to you, hasn't he?" she said. She looked over at Lawrence who was looking at John with a half-smile. Did Miss Renwick share John's sentiments? Surely she was anxious to put as much distance as possible between her and the disarray at Holywell House.

"I am sure," she said, watching John run ahead in a race with the dog, "that Mr. Foster and the other tenants are all breathing a large sigh of relief to have you in residence. It sounds as though the last landlord left much to be desired in his management."

Lawrence couldn't think what to respond to such a comment—hadn't she put together what a terrible landlord he was from what she had seen and heard? "Did you learn as much as you had hoped from Mr. Foster's conversation?"

"Yes," she responded with enthusiasm. "I found him to be very intelligent and well-acquainted with the particulars of the village and the land. Mr. Compton seems not to have realized just how fortunate he was in his bailiff. A sad and short-sighted waste of skill. Mr. Foster's ideas on new methods to increase the crops could be a boon to the estate if implemented."

Lawrence nodded slowly, thinking of the steward his father had hoped him to take on and wondering how he would stack up to someone like Mr. Foster who had years of experience besides the advantage of living in the village himself.

"He didn't say as much," Miss Renwick said, "but I assume that many of the villagers are discontent because of their experience with the last landlord. Did you hear when he mentioned that two good, hard-working families are reaching the end of their lease? I imagine they could be persuaded to stay by someone as capable and resourceful as yourself."

Lawrence whipped his head around to look at her. Was she teasing him? His parents had always lamented his lack of enterprise. "I'm not sure what you mean," he said.

She stared back at him, blinking as though his response was unexpected. "Someone with a creative mind like yours has an infinite resource at his disposal for solving the type of problems which must arise as the landlord of an estate like Holywell House. Besides," she added, not meeting his eye, "you solved a great problem for John and me when you took us in, though you were under no obligation to do so."

Lawrence opened his mouth and shut it again. He was so unused to the type of praise Miss Renwick was giving—not flattery or manipulation—genuine praise. He didn't recognize himself in what she was saying. When he thought on meeting the Renwicks at the inn and how he had decided to help them, he couldn't remember feeling that sense of obligation that he had become so sensitive to—the feeling that someone would be disappointed in him if he didn't comply. He had offered his help because he saw a need he knew he could satisfy, because it felt like the right thing to do.

He stole a glance at Miss Renwick. She was smiling as she looked down the lane where John was throwing a stick for Anne. John didn't want them to leave the next day.

And neither did Lawrence.

CHAPTER 7

*J*ohn declared himself to be famished when they reached Holywell House, and Eleanor sent what she felt was her hundredth—but surely not the last—apologetic glance at Mr. Debenham. He only smiled and then concurred with John, tugging on the bell with gusto once they had entered the drawing room.

Mr. Adley and Mr. Bower had ridden out on horseback, they were informed by the frazzled-looking housekeeper, so the three of them partook of the meats and cheese without them. Anne sat at John's feet, raising her head off the ground with beseeching eyes each time one of them set another serving on their plate.

Between John's unpredictable comments and Mr. Debenham's always-forbearing responses, Eleanor found a great deal of amusement in her company. She hadn't realized before how much difference there was in having an ally in her caretaking of John. Every time she worried about something John said or did, Mr. Debenham was quick to show her that her concern was unnecessary—that she could relax.

When she thought on where they might be if Mr. Debenham had

not taken pity on them at the inn, she felt a fresh wave of gratitude toward him—gratitude that he didn't wish to hear expressed.

He was an enigma to her in many ways. Lighthearted and easygoing, decidedly handsome, and yet there was a streak of disregard in him that she couldn't understand. The state of the home, his ignorance of all things relating to his tenants and farmland—they puzzled her. Based on what Mr. Adley and Mr. Bower had conveyed that morning, they had all been living a life devoted solely to their entertainment and comfort.

But she had seen the way Mr. Debenham's brow had become troubled as they walked through the village and as Farmer Foster's children innocently demonstrated the conditions they were living in, absent the care of Holywell House. Could he truly have been ignorant of what was expected of him as a landlord? It seemed impossible.

She watched with the hint of a smile, her mind only partially present, as Mr. Debenham and John argued over the merits of different cheeses, Mr. Debenham claiming victory when Anne chose his cheese over the one John had defended.

"Well," said Mr. Debenham once it was clear that they had all had their fill of the luncheon food, "I believe that a second room has been prepared for your use if you'd care to see it?"

John's head tilted to the side. "What's it like?"

"Like any other room, I should think," Mr. Debenham said, glancing at John who looked disappointed. He paused a moment then leaned toward John. "But next door to it is a room full of secrets," he said in a whisper. "We call it the Neverland room."

John's eyes widened like saucers. "Like the ship you told me about?"

Mr. Debenham nodded solemnly, and Eleanor took her lips between her teeth, trying not to smile. "Should you like to go see it?"

John nodded energetically, his eyes still round. He commanded Anne to stay and then followed Mr. Debenham from the room with Eleanor in their wake.

The hallway upstairs was dark even in the middle of a sunny day, the ivy providing a near-impenetrable barrier for the outdoor light. On a cloudy day such as this one, it was particularly dim and smelled of must. Mr. Debenham led them past the door to the room they had slept in, following the hallway past three more doors. He stopped in front of one and opened it, peeking in.

"This is the room that has been prepared for you," he said, moving so that John could look in. "Terribly boring, I'm afraid."

Eleanor came up behind John, placing a hand on each of his shoulders and looking into the room. It had two tall windows from which the curtains were pulled back, showing the outline of the green leaves which made a thick frame around them. There seemed to be an unusual number of candles in the room, placed on the hearth, the bedside table, the wardrobe, and the writing desk.

Eleanor glanced back at Mr. Debenham behind her, sending him a look of thanks. John was used to having plenty of light before bedtime, and it seemed Mr. Debenham had gathered as much.

"Plenty of candles," she said, "for further experimentation with shadows."

Mr. Debenham smiled. "Ah yes, I like an abundance of candles in my rooms, generally. I have somewhat of a reputation for my ability to create shadow creatures."

John's head whipped around. "Really?"

Mr. Debenham nodded. "Perhaps I can show you later this evening."

"I should like that above all things!" John said fervently.

Mr. Debenham closed the door and led them to the next room. He stopped in front of the door which was ajar and turned to John. "This is the Neverland room. You may be wondering why it is called that. Simply because, when I arrived here, this room had been left untouched by those who lived here before. They took nothing from the room, leaving it all to gather dust. Some of it is very mysterious. The servants have made mention of strange noises at night."

John looked as though he was itching to open the door himself. Mr. Debenham sent a mischievous half-smile at Eleanor and then opened the door as slowly as he could, delighting in the suspense that was apparent in the way John leaned forward.

The room was dim, the curtains pulled to with only a halo of light surrounding them where some of the light managed to seep through. Holland covers hung over some of the furniture, and the four-poster bed centered against the back wall had its maroon and gold curtains drawn.

John's neck turned as he scanned the room slowly. His shoulders slumped down. "This is nothing but an ordinary room!" he cried in a disillusioned voice.

Eleanor looked at him, biting her lip. He was right. There was nothing mysterious about the room beyond the cloth draped over some unknown pieces of furniture.

Mr. Debenham's brows went up, and he put a finger in front of his mouth to quiet them. He took a ginger step toward the bed, keeping his forefinger to his mouth. Eleanor felt her skin tingle as she watched his careful movements, and she noted the way John seemed to hold his body taut.

A floor board creaked under Mr. Debenham's feet, and he froze. Eleanor could feel herself stiffen. They were all still, listening for she knew not what. The air in the room suddenly seemed thick with anticipation, and the bits of light from the windows illuminated the dust that their presence had agitated, filling the place with a sense of mystery.

Mr. Debenham took another step toward the bed, reaching a hand toward the bed hangings and glancing backward toward John who inched a bit closer to Eleanor. Mr. Debenham ripped the hangings toward him, saying, "Ah ha!" John jumped toward Eleanor, and dust swirled around in the air.

The bed was empty, and Mr. Debenham relaxed his posture. "Hmm," he said, rubbing his bottom lip with his finger.

Eleanor looked at John whose eyes were narrowed. "It is just a regular old room after all!"

"Ah," said Mr. Debenham. "Perhaps so. Unless you have the eyes to see what lies beneath."

Eleanor smiled, but she felt her skin prickle nonetheless. Mr. Debenham had a way about him that was completely captivating. She almost found herself wishing she had the kind of eyes he spoke of.

He walked over to a large piece of furniture, shrouded by a holland cover and pulled it off, revealing a wardrobe. He opened the doors, revealing a number of garments and hats inside. He pulled a tricorne hat out and set it on his head.

Something fell to the side of the wardrobe, making a large clanking noise on the wooden floor. It was a cane. Mr. Debenham picked it up, inspecting it and running his hand along the polished wood. He suddenly jumped, spreading his legs into a fighting stance and pointing the cane at John and Eleanor who both reared back.

"So ye've come to Neverland, ay?" he said in the same pirate voice he had used at the stream. He reached behind him, keeping the cane pointed at them as he pulled out a hat and threw it to John who fumbled to catch it and then donned it.

He reached again and pulled out a long piece of purple fabric which he flung over to Eleanor. She reached to catch it and then held it up in confusion. A smaller, white piece of fabric dropped from within its folds.

She glanced at Mr. Debenham for guidance, and his shoulders shook as he shrugged. She tied the purple cloth around her waist like a belt and then reached for the white one, nonplussed.

Mr. Debenham dropped his sword and walked over, taking it from her hands and then moving behind her. She swallowed, unsure what to expect, electrically aware of his proximity. He wrapped the fabric around her forehead, tying it haphazardly on the side of her head. He put a hand on her shoulders and turned her toward him, inspecting his work with his bottom lip jutting out. She pursed her lips to stifle her smile as he nodded with decision and let go.

He strode back to his place and flipped around, pointing the cane at them again. "What are ye doing aboard Neverland?" he said. "Come to wrest the gold from the pirates, are ye?"

"Never!" John cried. "I'm a pirate, too!"

Mr. Debenham's lip trembled, but he said, "Well why didn't ye say so before? Come on over here!"

John rushed obediently to Mr. Debenham's side, turning to face Eleanor.

"And who might ye be, lass?" Mr. Debenham said to her. "Another pirate?"

"She's a traitor!" John cried. "She must be captured!"

Eleanor had only a split second to make a decision, but she chose to run toward the bed, with John and Mr. Debenham on her heels. She looked fiendishly for a way of escape, but there was nowhere to go but onto the bed.

She stopped short of it, turning around in time to see both John and Mr. Debenham just before her, and no time to prevent the resulting collision. She fell back onto the bed, John falling onto one side of her and Mr. Debenham onto the other.

Confusion ensued for a few moments, but John was the first to hop off, and he used his advantage to wrest the cane from Mr. Debenham's hand and level it at both him and Eleanor.

"Ha!" he cried. "Captured the traitor and the pirate! Now I may have all the gold for myself." He attempted a maniacal laugh.

Eleanor felt her shoulder resting against Mr. Debenham's arm, and her stomach flipped. She knew if she turned her head that his own would be only inches away.

"We've been caught, lass!" Mr. Debenham said. "Must we walk the plank then?"

"Aye!" cried John. "Follow me."

Eleanor felt Mr. Debenham sit up, taking the warmth from his arm with him. He extended both hands to her, a soft smile on his face, and she let him help her to a standing position. She looked down, adjusting the purple belt and brushing at her skirts which had accumulated dust.

They followed John out of the room and down the stairs toward the front door.

"I believe he means to take us back to the stream," Eleanor said.

Mr. Debenham laughed. "So he does."

Neither of them countered the plan, though, and silence reigned for a few moments between them as they followed the same matted-down path through the alfalfa.

The gratitude Eleanor had been feeling for Mr. Debenham's kindness toward them was quickly turning to regret. The time since their arrival at Holywell House felt much like a dream to her—one that would be too easily forgotten once they continued on their way home.

Since her mother's illness had set in, and even more significantly since her mother's death, Eleanor's life had been full of duty and obligation to her family. She had seen the way her father struggled to even show awareness of those around him, and so she had naturally tried to step in, particularly where John was concerned.

This time at Holywell House, though, had shown her a different reality than the one she was living—one with someone who somehow managed to turn her frustration with John into amusement. The burden of life had felt lighter in the presence of Mr. Debenham.

"He reminds me of myself at that age, you know," Mr. Debenham said, cutting in on her thoughts as he watched John whack at the alfalfa with the cane. "Full of imagination and energy."

"That he is," Eleanor replied. "I spend a great deal of time with him, and just watching him makes me wish for my bed some days. I wish I had the energy he does."

"So it is not just during your travel that you are caring for him?" Lawrence said, glancing at her. "I assumed that, at home, he would have a nursemaid or governess of some sort."

Eleanor smiled wryly. "He has had many a nursemaid and governess. But none of them have stayed with us long. The most recent one left just two weeks ago. John can be very difficult when he chooses to be."

"I can well imagine," Lawrence said as they watched John attack a particular patch of alfalfa with vigor. "So he drives them off in preference for your care?"

Eleanor nodded with a soft laugh. "He is simply too used to me to bear with someone new, I think. He always calls the women who come 'stuffy.' My father is beginning to think that I may be the only one who can undertake John's education for the time being. And I am glad to do it."

John called out to Lawrie, asking him to watch how strong he was, as evidenced by the way alfalfa went flying through the air with each swipe he took at it.

"I think," said Eleanor, "that he might worship you if we spend much more time here. All I hear is 'Lawrie, Lawrie, Lawrie.'" She took in a little breath, feeling strange at using his given name and wondering if she had given offense. Mr. Bower had made it clear that Mr. Debenham disliked the name.

Mr. Debenham was looking over at her, a strange expression on his face as he looked her in the eyes. He blew out a small laugh and shook his head, looking down.

"What is it?" she said.

He pursed his lips before answering. "I have always hated my name; always hated being called Lawrie—my father is also Lawrence, you see. But somehow you made it sound—" he paused and drew in a breath "—Well, it felt different."

Eleanor felt the heat seep into her cheeks. She wished she could ask him what he meant. "But plenty of men are called the same name as their father. Why should you hate it so?"

Mr. Debenham looked ahead of them, his eyes unfocused. "Because I don't want to become my father."

John whipped around to face them. "The plank!" He indicated the bridge with the cane in his hand.

Eleanor found herself feeling out of charity with John. She had so much more she wanted to ask Mr. Debenham. So much she wished to understand about him.

CHAPTER 8

The next day dawned as cloudy as had the prior day, and Lawrence looked through his ivy-veiled windows at the looming clouds with a frown. His mind had been taken up with Miss Renwick's situation as he tried to fall asleep. It seemed that she had been consigned to care for her younger brother for some time now. And yet, there was no evidence that she was frustrated by her situation.

Lawrence had difficulty imagining taking upon himself responsibility out of the goodness of his heart. He had never been given the choice, though. It had always been expected, always been drilled into him what he was duty-bound to do. He had complied for years, strived to meet the lofty expectations of his parents. But no matter how hard he tried, he seemed always to fall short.

So he had learned to fight against it and, in time, to give up entirely. That was what his time at Holywell House was. It was refusing to argue, refusing to exert the effort which he knew would be wasted.

But what if he chose to take on the responsibility himself, as Miss

Renwick had done? What if he did it, not out of obligation or to satisfy his parents, but rather because he wished to do it?

He finished tying his cravat and brushed off his sleeve, looking at himself in the mirror critically. It was time to decide exactly what he wanted in life.

Miss Renwick and John were already at the breakfast table when he went downstairs, John chatting animatedly with Mr. Adley and Mr. Bower. Mr. Adley had a hunted look on his face—he had never been one for much talk at the breakfast table—and Mr. Bower ate his food contentedly, showing no sign that he was even aware of being addressed by the boy.

Miss Renwick glanced up at Lawrence as he entered the room and smiled at him in greeting. He smiled in return, conscious of the way his heartbeat lost its rhythm at the sight of her.

"John, dear," she said, glancing at Mr. Adley with an apologetic smile as Lawrence seated himself, "some people prefer to eat their breakfast in silence."

"But why?" John said, puzzled.

"Not everyone begins the day with your level of enthusiasm, love."

"Regrettable, but true," Lawrence confirmed.

"Deb," said Mr. Adley, wiping his mouth with a napkin. "There's a letter for you on the tray over there." He gestured at the mahogany table that stood against the wall. "I believe," he said, his eyes watching Lawrence, "that it is from your father."

Lawrence stiffened. He hadn't heard from his parents in weeks—likely because he hadn't responded to their last letter inquiring after his work on the estate.

"Thank you," he said, trying to decide if he should even take the trouble of opening it. He could only imagine what its contents would be if his father was in communication with the steward Lawrence had been avoiding since his arrival. It couldn't be anything good.

"Did you ever find Mr. Foster's letters?" Miss Renwick asked.

Lawrence had forgotten about them entirely. He was not in the habit of reading letters at Holywell House, and his mind had been taken up with the Renwicks ever since their arrival. "No," he said, clenching his teeth in self-censure. "The thought slipped my mind somehow."

"Yes," Miss Renwick said, "well we have given you plenty to do and think on with our presence here, so I'm sure it's no surprise if you forgot."

Lawrence smiled and swallowed. She managed even to turn his inadequacies into praise. What would she do in his position? The house would surely not be in the state it was in, and no doubt she would have won over the hearts of all the tenants.

He thought on the Fosters and their roof. They had received rain during the night, and Lawrence clenched his teeth as he thought of what that must have meant for the leaking roofs. And all when a simple fix such as rethatching would improve their living conditions so considerably.

He stood suddenly, causing the table to jolt. Mr. Bower's head shot up at the disturbance. He looked at Lawrence with his brows raised and a smudge of preserves on his chin. "What are you doing?"

"I'm leaving," Lawrence replied, scooting his chair in.

"Can't leave," Mr. Bower said, looking at Lawrence's plate which had two untouched pieces of toast and a cup full of ale beside it. "Haven't eaten a morsel."

Lawrence looked at the food on his plate and pursed his lips before glancing at the dog. "Give it to Anne," he said. "I'm going into the village."

"Whatever for?" Mr. Adley asked.

"Can I come?" said John.

"The roofs need thatching," he replied, glancing outside, "and by the looks of it, we'll be receiving more rain today." He knew the idea would sound mad to his friends. But he needed to show the tenants he meant to do better by them than he had been. And that would require some work.

John insisted on accompanying him, while Mr. Adley and Mr.

Bower exchanged significant glances of concern for Lawrence. When Lawrence offered to take John with him alone, Miss Renwick shook her head.

"I should like to come help if I may. I only need a few minutes to change, if that's all right with you." She looked a question at him.

Who was this woman? He smiled and nodded at her. "Of course."

His friends exchanged more looks full of meaning. "Perhaps we should come along as well," Mr. Adley said doubtfully.

Lawrence's brows shot up, and Mr. Bower nodded vigorously. "Don't wish to be made to look nohow when even Miss Renwick insists on helping."

The five of them—six including Anne—set off in a matter of thirty minutes for the village. The commands Lawrence had issued to his servants had been executed swiftly if with raised brows, and the group walked down the lane with two wheelbarrows, one guided by John's unsteady hands and the other by Lawrence.

The expression on Mr. Foster's face when they arrived was enough to confirm Lawrence in his somewhat spontaneous decision to help—the man was shocked. Thanks to the haymaking efforts of his family over the past few weeks, Mr. Foster had a large store laid up, and though he had plans to sell most of it to the nearest town, Lawrence assured him that he would pay him for it directly.

The straw was brought around to the village lane in the wheelbarrows, and Lawrence found himself on the roof with Mr. Foster and John, learning how to replenish the thatching. Much of the existing straw was in a bad state and needed replacing. Lawrence realized that he had his work cut out for him. It wasn't long, though before the surrounding tenants began to spill out of their homes and offer their assistance.

With the gray clouds above moving swiftly toward a deeper blue, the scent in the air was a mixture of humid, approaching rain and wheat straw. Lawrence found himself sweating from the humid air but blessing the cloud cover that blocked the heat of the sun which would otherwise have been beating down upon them.

Near the end of the day, Lawrence stood up straight on the roof, stretching his aching muscles and looking over to where Mr. Adley and Mr. Bower stood bent over on the roof two houses down, adding to the thatching. He smiled to himself. Never did he think to see the two of them engaged in such manual labor. Mr. Bower had proven to be quite skilled in the work—a fact which had taken Lawrence by surprise. There was much more to Mr. Bower than met the eye or ear.

John had left with some of the village children to play in the stream, Anne on his heels and the Colonel in his hand. Miss Renwick was on the ground below holding a pitchfork with a pile of straw beside her. Lawrence moved carefully down the roof, feeling grateful that the roofs weren't more sloped.

"Are you as famished as I am, Miss Renwick? I believe your work is harder than mine has been."

She smiled up at him, wiping her brow. "I admit to feeling a fair amount of hunger."

Lawrence gazed over at the other men. "I believe we've nearly finished. I instructed Mrs. O'Keefe to prepare an early dinner for us, as I anticipated that we would wish for it earlier than usual."

One of the older village boys who had stayed behind to work fetched John at the stream, and the group of them walked back to Holywell House with tired limbs, aching backs, and the genuine thanks of the entire village. Light raindrops began falling as they reached the overgrown courtyard of Holywell House.

CHAPTER 9

*L*awrence sat back in his chair, sipping his glass, listening to Mr. Adley and Mr. Bower go back and forth across the table, joking about Lawrence knew not what. How many times had they sat over this same table, the room filled with the sound of raucous laughter and the smell of port and brandy? Too many times to count. It had always ended in a game of cards.

But tonight, Lawrence wasn't thinking on cards. He was thinking on the Renwicks, feeling anxious to join them in the drawing room, feeling an ennuie that he hadn't felt since coming to Holywell House.

A candle near one of the French doors flickered, and Lawrence stood to go close the door that stood ajar, letting the cool breeze of a night turning windy into the warm room.

He glanced at the candle, thinking on all the candles he had ordered to be placed in the guest room John would be sleeping in. He had been afraid of the dark as a boy, too—always dreading the moment when the candle would be snuffed out by the nurse, leaving him to the darker side of his imagination which inevitably plagued him before sleep saved him.

The expression Miss Renwick had worn on seeing the multitude of candles—warm appreciation—had ignited something inside him, a feeling that he had struggled to put a name to. He had told her before not to bother expressing her thanks to him, but somehow she managed to convey it by the way she smiled at him whenever he humored John, whenever he showed the least kindness to them.

He had never learned to accept thanks with grace—probably because he was rarely shown appreciation at home. What he did was never quite enough to meet his parents' expectations. And yet Miss Renwick, after such a short time knowing him, had managed to praise him, thank him, and encourage all the better parts of him—parts he hadn't even known existed outside of a desire to please his parents.

But exist they did. He found great fulfillment in helping the Renwicks, in making them as comfortable as he could in this miserable house. He found that he craved the company of the Renwicks—Miss Renwick in particular. He wished to know what had brought her, unchaperoned, to the area, with a rambunctious little brother in tow—one she seemed to be accustomed to having charge of.

"Eh, Deb?" Mr. Adley's voice cut in on his thoughts.

He turned toward him, brows raised in a question. "What, now?"

"The Renwicks," Mr. Adley said with a touch of impatience. "They leave tomorrow?"

"That is the plan, I believe," he replied, trying to ignore the way he felt as he confirmed the question. He cleared his throat. "The wind is picking up, and I believe the doors to be open in the drawing room as well. I shall go make sure they are closed."

Mr. Bower's eyes were trained on him, but it was Mr. Adley who said, "Whatever for? Send a servant."

"The two of them have enough to do as is," he said, striding toward the door.

His opening of the drawing room door went unnoticed at first, and he had to put a fist to his mouth to stifle the laugh that tried to burst through at the picture presented.

Miss Renwick, dressed in a pale blue sarsnet dress, grabbed for a pillow from the settee behind her as John pointed a fireplace poker at her. He was distracted, though, trying to force Anne to allow him to ride on her back, an idea the dog seemed not at all fond of.

"What is this?" Lawrence said, thinking he had better intervene sooner than later. Miss Renwick's head came around, a look of relief on her face.

"John has assured me that I must suffer retribution for my treacherous acts against the pirates of Neverland."

"Good heavens!" Lawrence said, running over to John and taking the poker from him gently but with a firm hand. "You must know that this is not the way retribution is doled out, good man. Not on Neverland, at least."

John looked up at him, curious. "How is it doled out?"

Lawrence considered, searching for a quick answer that would satisfy the boy but also keep Miss Renwick safe from any future imaginary treachery.

"Poison," he blurted out.

John drew back a little, and Lawrence could see Miss Renwick's brows shoot up in his peripheral vision.

"That's right," he continued. He set the poker stick next to the fireplace and walked over to the table which held the tea tray. He made a showy gesture toward it. "This is the poison she must drink." He saw the lines appear at the corner of Miss Renwick's dancing eyes, along with the smile of gratitude he had come to associate with her.

"Tea?" John said with a doubtful look.

"Ah," Lawrence said, putting up a finger. "To the untrained eye, yes, it bears no small resemblance toward regular tea. But it is the most vile poison imaginable, made all the more vile with the use of these—" he indicated the sugar and then the cream. "It takes some time to perfect the ratios, so I encourage you to get to work."

John rushed over, sitting down in front of the tray and rubbing his hands together as he scanned the materials available to him.

Lawrence looked over at Eleanor who was covering her mouth

with a hand, her eyes sparkling above with amusement. He walked over to her side, turning to watch John as he poured tea in a saucer.

"I believe you have saved my life, Mr. Debenham," she said, leaning over to him to avoid her voice carrying to John.

"Have I?" he said, sending her a look full of meaning before he indicated John with his head.

She smiled and looked to her brother who was dropping lump after lump of sugar in the teacup. "True. By all accounts, this concoction looks to be fatal."

He laughed as he pulled the French doors closed and then indicated the settee behind Miss Renwick, inviting her to sit. She took a seat on the far end, and he was conscious of a feeling of disappointment. Had she seated herself in the middle, he would have had an excuse to sit himself in closer proximity to her. As it was, he sat on the opposite end.

"Is he always this determined?" Lawrence asked, watching John pour cream into the tea with a look of intense focus.

"I'm afraid so," Miss Renwick answered.

Lawrence smiled. "It must be exhausting. I imagine you will be relieved to hand him off to someone else when you arrive in Attleborough."

John spilled a teaspoon of cream on the floor, and Lawrence put out a hand to stop Miss Renwick from going to attend to the mess.

She closed her eyes as if to summon patience for her brother. "The challenge will be to find a new nursemaid for John once we arrive, given his habit of driving them away. His care will fall to me until we can find someone suitable. I hope that the new surroundings will capture his fancy enough to keep away the sullens, for he is quite pleasant as long as he is happy and busy."

"I can well imagine," Lawrence replied. "Where were you before? Was it not to your father's taste?"

Miss Renwick swallowed and wet her lips. "Not exactly. We lived in Kent, but once my mother passed two years ago, it became too painful to my father to continue there."

Lawrence clenched his fist, wishing he could hit himself for bringing up a topic bound to be painful. "I am so sorry, Miss Renwick."

She smiled softly. "Thank you. I think it is for the best, our moving."

Lawrence found himself in agreement. The thought of being deprived of the Renwick's company and acquaintance had they stayed in Kent was not one he wished to dwell on. How had he come to feel so attached to them in such a short time?

Miss Renwick's hand shot out to his, pointing his attention toward John who was holding out a teaspoon full of his concoction toward Anne. She sniffed at it and then lapped up with her tongue what she could.

Lawrence nodded his approval. "Naturally he must confirm that it is indeed a mortal brew before forcing you to swallow it."

Anne sat back on her hind legs and waited patiently for more. John's bottom lip jutted out, and he shook his head before pouring an entirely new cup, clearly dissatisfied with what he had created.

"It seems," Lawrence said, leaning over and whispering, "that your death sentence has been mercifully delayed."

Miss Renwick heaved a feigned sigh of relief. "What a comfort! There is so much I have yet to do and see in the world."

"More London Seasons?" he teased.

"Or a first, perhaps," Miss Renwick replied, her voice soft.

He turned toward her, an arrested expression on his face. "You've not had a Season?"

She shook her head, but her eyes stayed on John.

"Then I must find a way to stop your poisoning," he said, hoping to lighten the mood. His brows came together. "I was sure you were out."

The smile he had been hoping for appeared on Miss Renwick's face. "I believe I should take offense at your words, Mr. Debenham— the implication being that I appear too old not to be out."

He drew back, horrified at her inference, but she only laughed at his reaction. "You are right, however. I should have been out many Seasons ago." She paused a moment. "I was needed at home, though, during my mother's illness."

And then she would have been in mourning after her mother's death. "For John?" he asked, the softness of his voice matching hers.

Her smile widened as she watched John stir the tea in front of him, his brow wrinkled in focus. "Yes, for him, for my mother, and for my father."

Lawrence stifled the impulse to shudder. What would he have done if his own future had been put on hold for his family? For his parents? "You have sacrificed much of yourself for your family, then."

"Perhaps," she said. "But I have also found a great deal of joy and fulfillment in helping bear my father's burden and in ensuring that John is taken care of." She looked at him with her brows raised. "That wasn't always true, though. I found early on in my mother's illness that I was beginning to resent my family and my mother's situation for what I felt deprived of.

"I fought it for a period and was miserable; I was convinced that I was oppressed. It was only with time that I realized that changing my thoughts could change how happy I was. I discovered that it served me better to think of my duties as opportunities rather than burdens. I had to do these things no matter what, true. But I could choose to do them happily or grudgingly.

"So I began to do things before being asked. And slowly, I found myself treasuring the moments of caring for my mother, enjoying more of my time with John—though sometimes I wish to box his ears soundly." She glanced over at John with a warm smile. "I am very fond of John. Our time here has reminded me of that forcefully."

Lawrence chewed the inside of his lip. There was no bitterness in her voice, no resentment. Somehow she seemed to have peace despite a life full of the obligation Lawrence so despised and avoided.

Miss Renwick let out a large sigh and looked over at Lawrence with a grimace tempered by the smile quivering behind it. "I believe my time has come." She took the teacup which John offered to her on its saucer. "I bid you all adieu." A crack of thunder sounded outside, and Miss Renwick gave him a significant glance as though it portended her fate.

Lawrence chuckled softly as she sipped the tea, but her words brought a lump to his throat. Tomorrow would indeed be adieu.

~

THE LONG SUMMER days meant that the light was only fading to sunset at nine. Miss Renwick had left the drawing room with John a half hour before, telling him to prepare for bedtime. Though she had instantly fallen over after her first sip of tea—a convincing, vacant expression on her face belied only by the slightest tremor at the corner of her mouth—she seemed to have recovered fully since then, a fact which John seemed not to mind, despite his focused efforts at creating a fatal mixture.

Lawrence lingered in the drawing room for a time, awaiting his friends who seemed to be lingering a great while over their port. No doubt they were discussing Lawrence's strange behavior since the Renwicks' arrival.

He sighed and stood, thinking he would turn in early after such a tiring day. His limbs were exhausted, but he felt surprisingly content. He had felt a great sense of fulfillment as they walked down the village lane, seeing the full and fresh thatching on all the roofs.

He removed his jacket, looking out his window where dusk was setting in. Rain began to pound, and the fading light was punctuated by flashes of bright lightning.

An urgent knock sounded on his door, and he tossed his cravat onto the nearest chair, his brow knitted. Who in the world?

He opened the door, and Miss Renwick stood before him, wringing her hands, her eyes frantic.

"What is it?" he said.

"Have you seen John?" she asked. She swallowed, glancing down the hallway which Lawrence had asked be lit with candles.

He shook his head. "I thought he would be in bed?"

Miss Renwick shook her head. "I believed him to be settling in as well, but he is not in his room, nor is Anne."

Lawrence tried to push down the tingling fear he began to feel. "Have you checked the Neverland room?"

She nodded. "And the drawing room and dining room. Mr. Adley and Mr. Bower haven't seen him either." She paused, swallowing again. "I am afraid that he has gone in search of the Colonel. He asked me when I left him at his room if I had seen the toy, and I told him to think on where he last had it." Thunder sounded, and her lip trembled slightly. She put a hand to it. "The last time I saw him with it was in the village when he went with the children to the stream."

Lawrence swore softly. The pounding rain and fading light would not help in the search. "Let me get my jacket." He rushed to his wardrobe, taking out his brown greatcoat which he flung on.

"I am coming with you," Miss Renwick said, her voice breaking.

Lawrence put his hands on her shoulders, looking her in the eyes frankly. He hated seeing her in such an apprehensive state. "I shan't try to dissuade you if it's what you wish. But I would strongly advise you to remain here. If he is indeed outdoors, we will need to be prepared here to warm and dry him. Instruct Mrs. O'Keefe to prepare some broth or gruel."

A flash of lightning illuminated the doorway where they stood. "I must go," he said, trying to rid his mind of the image of John in the open fields during such lightning strikes.

CHAPTER 10

$\mathcal{E}$leanor stood rooted to the spot for a moment after Mr. Debenham left. Her mind kept taking her terrible places, with visions of John's lifeless form coming through the door in Mr. Debenham's arms. She had never considered that John would take her careless words as a suggestion to go off on his own and find the Colonel. How she wished she could go back to that conversation and redo it!

She sprang into action. She needed to be ready when Mr. Debenham returned. She didn't know whether to wish for him to find John or not, for it would mean that John was indeed outside at a time when the elements were at their most dangerous. She descended the stairs with rushed footsteps, calling out for Mrs. O'Keefe and tugging the nearest bell pull multiple times.

She readied the extra pair of clothes from John's portmanteau, folded two blankets to bring downstairs, and instructed the house-keeper to make broth and have towels and a warm bath ready.

After her preparations, time seemed to tick by agonizingly slowly. She sat on the edge of the settee, glancing at the long-case clock again and again, only to see the hands showing 6:08. It had not been wound for some time, if Mr. Bower had spoken correctly.

The fifth time she glanced up at it, she let out a frustrated sigh and stood, walking swiftly over and looking around for the key. It sat upon the nearby mantle, covered in a coat of dust which she blew off, pulling her head away to avoid the musty cloud which puffed off it.

She wound the clock, approximating the time as best she could based on when the sun had set. Having accomplished that, she sat down again, her anxious hands pulling at a stray thread on her dress.

It had been at least half an hour since Mr. Debenham had left, and each minute seemed to portend a worse fate for John. Eleanor shook her head and shut her eyes, trying to ignore the nightmarish visions her mind insisted on conjuring.

If only they had never gone to the stream! Surely the rains had made the quaint, gurgling waters surge, saturated with dirt and sticks. What if John had tried to cross the bridge again and slipped? What if Mr. Debenham was injured or even struck by lightning as he searched?

Lightning flashed in the windows, briefly illuminating the landscape outside with the sheets of rain slanting at an angle from the wind. Eleanor suppressed a shudder just as a crash sounded, nearly drowned in the noise of thunder.

Eleanor jumped up, recognizing the sound as the front door swinging open. She rushed to the door of the drawing room and into the hall. Mr. Debenham was carrying John whose head lolled back. She sighed as she saw the Colonel, rising up and down on John's chest.

A lump rose in Eleanor's throat, and she felt faint. It took a moment for her to realize that the skinny, black creature which slipped into the house was Anne.

"In here," she called to Mr. Debenham over the din of rain falling on the courtyard's pebbled drive.

His hair was matted to his forehead, rain dripping down in rivulets all over his face, and his clothes were soaked.

He rushed past her, saying breathlessly, "Call for the doctor."

Eleanor ignored the way her head felt light, and she tugged on the bell, returning to John who Mr. Debenham had laid on the settee. Eleanor put a pillow under his head and went to retrieve the clothing, blankets, and towels which sat on two chairs against the wall.

"I believe he has injured his arm. I only found him thanks to Anne. Her bark led me to him, on the edge of the stream near the whirlpool. I think Anne must have pulled him to shore from the way he was positioned and by the state of his hair." He took in a breath.

Eleanor felt a tear trail down her cheek, and motioned for Anne to come over, stroking her wet fur and saying, "Good girl."

The doctor was sent for, and Eleanor and Mr. Debenham worked to take off the wet clothing which was plastered to John's body, drying him with towels and then covering him with blankets. His injured arm they let be, and it hung awkwardly on the settee cushion.

Eleanor's heart raced without slowing as they worked. Every time she looked at John's unconscious face, she swallowed painfully.

Mr. Debenham reached for her hand, and she looked up at him, her eyes filling as she met his. "He will be all right." He squeezed her hand, and she smiled weakly, grateful for his reassurance, no matter how difficult she found it to believe.

The doctor arrived and examined John, praising Eleanor and Mr. Debenham for their wise action in warming and drying him. He confirmed that he would need to set the bone and that it was best done while John was still unconscious. He took a vial of laudanum out of his bag, pouring some into John's mouth.

"Be at peace," he said to them. "I set many an arm during my days as a surgeon in the war."

Eleanor watched in apprehension as he prepared to set the bone. Mr. Debenham stood next to her, his jaw set. Nothing could have prepared Eleanor, though, for the agonizing cry John let out when the deed was performed. She bit her lip and grabbed for Mr. Debenham's hand which he clasped tightly.

John continued to cry out, reaching for his injured arm, and the doctor asked Mr. Debenham to hold John's uninjured arm down. Eleanor released Mr. Debenham's hand and turned her head away, her fist in front of her mouth. She reminded herself that John was at least alive and conscious, a fact she should find great comfort in.

After the doctor attached a wood splint to John's arm, his cries turned to whimpers, and the doctor finally nodded to Eleanor. She rushed over, kneeling next to the settee and wiping at her tears as she reassured John that she was there with him.

"It was by no means the worst break I have seen," the doctor said. "He will need this, though—" he handed the laudanum vial to Eleanor "—and I shall return tomorrow to see how he goes on."

He gave a few final instructions to Mr. Debenham and left.

"He says we may move him to his bed, but we must naturally take the greatest care in doing so."

John's eyes were red, the lids hanging heavily. "Nell?" he said in a weak voice.

"Yes, love?" She stroked his wet hair away from his face.

"May I sleep with you tonight?"

She swallowed the lump in her throat and nodded. "Of course."

Mr. Debenham carried him up to Eleanor's bed with gentle strength, setting him down under the covers which Eleanor had pulled back.

After seeing that he was settled, Mr. Debenham bent down next to John. "Well, my good man, I shall leave you to rest. I suppose we must hold off on any sword fights until your arm is mended."

John tried to reject the idea, but it came out weak. "I can fight with my left hand, just like any good pirate."

Mr. Debenham chuckled and mussed John's hair. Eleanor smiled at the interaction. Mr. Debenham had been a godsend in so many ways, and it was oddly satisfying to watch their interaction.

Mr. Debenham stood up straight and turned to leave.

"Lawrie?" John's raspy voice called.

Mr. Debenham turned, his brows raised in a question.

"Can you tell me a story?"

Eleanor took her lips between her teeth. Mr. Debenham looked exhausted, and he was still wet from going out to search for John. With his damp hair, tired eyes, and the clinging white shirt with its collar hanging limply around his neck, Eleanor had never found him more handsome. He had saved John's life, and his appearance showed it.

He smiled weakly and walked back over to the bed, sitting on the edge, his body turned toward John. Eleanor sat on the other side, holding John's injured hand lightly in hers, making sure not to disturb the splint. She met eyes with Mr. Debenham, wishing she could convey the depth and breadth of her gratitude toward him; the way she had so quickly come to rely on his presence.

He didn't smile as he returned her gaze. His eyes held hers steadily for a pregnant moment, and Eleanor felt as though a string had been pulled taut between them, connecting them.

"Will you tell me more tales of Neverland?" John asked.

Mr. Debenham nodded and began a new tale, one of his hands resting on the bed as John listened with drooping lids. Slowly the lids closed, and, in what seemed an unconscious gesture, his hand reached out for Mr. Debenham's, holding it just as he held Eleanor's.

Mr. Debenham stopped talking, his expression surprised.

Eleanor met his gaze, a soft smile on her face. "He is so very fond of you," she said in a soft voice. "You have been so kind to him."

He shook his head as if to shake away her gratitude. "I have become quite fond of him, as well." He looked at John whose chest was rising and falling steadily.

Eleanor bit her lip. John's injury meant they would not be able to continue their journey home the following day, even if the repair was done. She would have to write her father to let him know of the delay.

"I hope," she said, "to hear from our coachman tomorrow about the repair to the wheel. We have imposed upon you enough, and I think John can make the trip back to the inn with minimal suffering if the carriage is ready."

Mr. Debenham shook his head again, this time emphatically. "It does not even bear considering. You must stay here until he is well enough to travel, carriage or no."

She looked into his eyes, trying to decipher his thoughts. Was he simply being civil? The relief she felt at his offer was due, in part, to the knowledge that she wouldn't have to transport John to the village, for they couldn't possibly travel on the wet roads toward home when he was in such a state. They would have to seek accommodations in town, facing yet again the probability that there were none to be had.

But the other part of her relief was, she had to acknowledge, for the knowledge that she would not have to say goodbye to Mr. Debenham quite yet. The prospect of a future without his presence made her throat feel tight.

He met her gaze without wavering, a soft light gleaming in his as he watched her.

She sighed. "I would be dishonest if I didn't admit to feeling relief at the prospect of remaining here a little longer. Just until John has had a couple of days to rest. It is so kind of you to offer it."

He smiled wryly. "What makes you sure that my offer isn't an entirely selfish desire for time with you?"

She felt warmth creep into her neck and cheeks. Did he mean with her or with both her and John? Surely the latter. She couldn't allow herself to hope he meant the former.

JOHN PASSED A DIFFICULT NIGHT, tossing and turning, complaining of the pain in his arm despite the laudanum Eleanor made sure to give him periodically. After two hours of attempted—and unsuccessful—sleep, Eleanor moved to the makeshift bed which still sat on the floor of the room.

John awoke ornery, and though Eleanor understood that it was due to his injury, her lack of sleep made her particularly short on patience. When a knock sounded on the door mid-morning to reveal Mr. Debenham, she knew she looked as frazzled as she felt.

Upon seeing her, his expression morphed from kind to concerned.

"I don't want gruel!" John shouted from behind Eleanor. "I want real food. Can't you see I'm fair gutfounded, Nell?"

Eleanor bit her lip to stifle her smile—both at John's use of a cant expression and at Mr. Debenham's surprise on hearing it. "I believe he learned a number of phrases from Mr. Adley yesterday, and he has been demonstrating them all morning."

Mr. Debenham attempted a grimace, but he chuckled, glancing at John and then back to Eleanor. "Go take a break," he said. "I shall stay with him awhile."

Eleanor battled for a moment, but in the end, she accepted the offer. She needed some time to gather her thoughts and get a better hold on her temper.

She headed straight for the stairs once Mr. Debenham had exchanged places with her and from there to the front door. The day had dawned cool but sunny, and the outdoors seemed the best place to find some serenity. She walked around the house to the rear where the gardens sat—or at least would have if they had been maintained.

The boxwood hedges were uneven and overgrown, and the flower beds within them a mixture of plants which were dead and others which had overrun the beds. Weeds poked up from the dirt path. The long, narrow pool of water was covered in a blanket of green moss, the water beneath showing through in murky patches.

Eleanor found a stone bench which had barely enough room for one seat due to the crowding of the shrubbery surrounding it.

She had no idea what to make of her current position. She regretted coming to Holywell House, but whether it was because she truly wished they had never come or that she wished they never need leave, she didn't know.

She didn't know whether to look on Mr. Debenham as the

preserver of John's life or the cause of his injury. He was fun-loving—perhaps to a fault. He had neglected his estate and his tenants for months, and for what reason? The tales he told of Neverland at times seemed to Eleanor to reveal just how much time he spent living in an imaginary world—somewhat like John did.

And yet, despite it all, she was swiftly falling in love with the man.

CHAPTER 11

*L*awrence closed the door behind him, taking in a deep breath as the door shut. He had managed to persuade John to eat the gruel, but it had not been without difficulty.

It had taken all of his imagination to concoct a scenario in which a pirate would need to eat gruel. Had Miss Renwick been dealing with John being out of sorts since he had left the night before? Only a saint could deal with such taciturnity all day, every day.

He didn't mistake Miss Renwick for a saint, per se. But he found himself looking for excuses to seek her out and to help her. The races at Newmarket which would begin the next day—something Lawrence had been looking forward to since his arrival at Holywell House—seemed not only trivial but a waste of time he could be spending with the Renwicks.

He had tried to convince himself that it was John's naive and energetic personality which drew him to them. But he could only hide his feeling under that mask for so long—not when he found so much joy and fulfillment in Miss Renwick's company even when John was engaged in his childish antics.

Where had Miss Renwick gone since she had left him with John?

Perhaps she was taking a well-deserved nap in John's room. Or perhaps she had chosen to sleep in the Neverland room bed.

A half-smile appeared on his face as he thought of John forcing them to stay fixed on the bed as he exulted in their capture and pointed the cane at them. Every time he was in the same room with Miss Renwick, he had the odd sensation as if there were some sort of magnet between them. The closer they were, the stronger it felt, and they had never been closer than when they had tumbled onto that bed.

He took in another deep breath and pushed open the door to the drawing room. Mr. Adley and Mr. Bower sat at the table, partaking of a late breakfast. They had already consumed the bottles of brandy Lawrence had bought from Mr. Jeffers at the inn and so had gone into town to the pub after dinner. They had not even invited Lawrence to join them, and it had bothered him slightly when he discovered where they had gone. He felt distant from them since the Renwicks arrival, and he didn't know what to make of it.

"Has Miss Renwick been down this morning?" he asked.

Mr. Adley and Mr. Bower exchanged significant glances. "Good morning to you, too, Deb," said Adley.

Lawrence shook his head and rubbed at his eyes. "I'm sorry. John was injured last night in the storm, and my mind is all over the place."

Mr. Adley raised his brows as he lowered his head to his food. "Could have fooled me. I've thought your mind was in one very particular place for the last few days."

"What does that mean?" Lawrence said, his brows snapping together.

Mr. Adley was silent, but Mr. Bower chimed in. "Miss Renwick," he said without looking up from his food. "He thinks you've formed a tendre for her. So do I, come to think of it. Plain as a pikestaff."

Lawrence swallowed. "Nonsense," he said, walking over to the side board as a form of distraction. He had no intention of speaking to Adley and Bower about his regard for Miss Renwick. He didn't need them to remind him that to marry would be a surrender to his parents' expectations.

He looked at the letter tray. One sealed letter sat on it, and Lawrence recognized the script of his father. In the events of the day before, he had forgotten that he had a letter from his parents.

He sat looking at it and became aware of a ticking noise. He picked up the letter and walked to the long-case clock. The hands moved, keeping time for the first time since he had arrived. He stared at it for a moment.

"Apparently Miss Renwick wound it last night," Mr. Adley said in a disinterested voice.

Lawrence's gaze rested on the clock a moment longer before he opened the sealed letter with the knife on the nearby tray.

His eyes moved swiftly along the neatly-written lines of the page-long missive, and he felt his pulse begin to throb in his neck, the over-powering anger which he hadn't felt since last being in his father's presence beginning to consume him. It was the unquestioning assumption that Lawrence would comply with the demands his father made—demands he hadn't even taken the time to veil as requests.

So much for letting Lawrence take over the management of Holy-well House. It was the unabashed encouragement for him to marry a responsible woman of good stock as soon as he could. But most of all, it was how his father conveyed their intention to come visit and see how Lawrence was faring which sent him over the edge.

He refused to listen to his parents criticize him in person at the estate that they had forced onto him. He heard the ticking of the clock, and it seemed to synchronize with his pulse. Suddenly Miss Renwick's winding of the clock seemed a gross encroachment—yet another person trying to force order upon him.

He stalked out of the room and out the front door, his long strides cutting through the weed-filled courtyard. He couldn't respond to his father's letter, telling them not to come. If he knew them at all, they were already on their way from Coventry. He must either confront them in person or avoid them—leave to Adley or Bower's house, perhaps.

He came up short. His aimless walk had brought him into the gardens, and Miss Renwick was kneeling on the ground some ten feet away, her hands reaching into one of the overgrown flower beds.

She looked up at him with a smile, wiping her forehead with the back of her forearm. She froze on seeing Lawrence's face.

"What is wrong?" she said, struggling to stand quickly, wiping her ungloved hands on her dirt-splotched dress. "Is it John?"

Lawrence shook his head, looking at her and then to the pile of weeds she stood beside. "I thought you were going to rest," he said in a colorless voice.

She followed his gaze to the pile of weeds. "I came outside for some fresh air, to try to escape my fretting over John, and somehow I found that I needed to busy my hands."

He didn't move. She was winding the clocks, weeding the flower beds—trying to fix everything she saw wrong with him and how he was living.

Her cheeks began to take on a pink hue, deepening to crimson. "I am so sorry," she said, looking at the flower bed she had been working in. "I wasn't even thinking. I should have asked you before doing such a thing."

"Yes," he said, trying to keep his voice steady. "Perhaps you should have asked before winding the clock, as well."

Her eyes widened, and she swallowed, a conscience-stricken look on her face. "I apologize. I was agonizing as I waited for you to return last night, worrying that something had gone terribly wrong with John, or perhaps even with you...." She trailed off, looking away. "It doesn't matter. It was wrong of me, and I am sorry."

Lawrence's jaw shifted from side to side. He wanted to be angry with her, but she had taken the wind out of his sails. The winding of the clock, her weeding in the garden—they had both been done as a result of the concern she had felt, the difficulties she was laboring through. She couldn't help herself; her responsible nature seemed to instinctively lead her to create order out of chaos when she was under stress. She was precisely the type of woman his parents would wish him to marry.

"John wishes to see you," he said.

She glanced at him quickly, looked down at the weeds beside her, and picked the pile up into her arms, walking past him with a mortified expression on her face, avoiding his eyes.

He stood still after she had left, his jaw beginning to ache from the exertion of clenching it as he had been. He should have offered to carry the pile of dead plants for her. He should not have made her feel bad. He didn't seem to be able to do anything right.

THE FOLLOWING DAY, Lawrence barely saw Miss Renwick. Lawrence tried not to pay mind to the disappointment he felt upon entering the drawing room, only to see his friends. She seemed to have breakfasted early and then returned to care for John. No doubt she was avoiding Lawrence. Perhaps it was for the best. Lawrence had a sneaking suspicion that, should he spend any more time with Miss Renwick than he had, he would likely waver in his determination to disregard his feelings for her.

As angry as he had been in the gardens, he had known an impulse to go over to her and apologize, to make plain his feelings. But his thoughts turned to his father's letter, and his ire flared up again. Would he throw away all the work to establish his independence from his parents after such a short acquaintance with a woman?

The expected letter from the Renwick's coachman arrived just after breakfast. Lawrence had half a mind to send Mrs. O'Keefe to deliver it, but he ignored the impulse, wishing to know what Miss Renwick's plan was and how John was faring.

He scaled the stairs slowly, steeling himself against the impending interaction, and knocked softly on the bedroom door. He could hear John's voice inside, much less petulant than the day before. That was a good sign for his recovery.

The door opened, and Miss Renwick blinked twice on seeing Lawrence, her mouth opening slightly but wordlessly. He looked past her toward John, trying to ignore the way he could see the hurt in Miss Renwick's eyes.

He greeted John who raised his splinted arm joyfully in salutation.

"Lawrie!" he cried. "Where have you been?"

Lawrence forced a smile. Trust John to bring to the forefront the subject he was hoping to avoid. "I've been remiss, haven't I? I've been a bit taken up with various things—I apologize." He looked to Miss Renwick, noting the way the morning light which poured through the window behind framed her with a sort of halo. "I've come to give you this." He handed her the letter. "I believe it is from your coachman."

Miss Renwick took it from him and broke the seal, anxiously reading the contents. Lawrence waited, biting the inside of his lip.

She folded it back up, not meeting Lawrence's eyes. "The carriage wheel is repaired. He informs us that he will await us at the inn in town unless he hears from me instructing him to come here directly."

Lawrence nodded, wishing she would look up at him—it was too easy to forget the exact shade of blue in her eyes. "Well, you must know that my own carriage is at your disposal whenever you have need of it."

"Are you going to come visit, Lawrie?" John's voice piped up from behind.

Lawrence saw Miss Renwick close her eyes in a gesture of forbearance, and he cleared his throat. "In fact, I have plans to leave shortly for Mr. Adley's estate."

John's pout made an appearance.

Lawrence looked at Miss Renwick again. "But you are both welcome here as long as you need somewhere to stay."

Miss Renwick looked at him for the first time, a weak smile on her lips. "Thank you," she said, "but I think we shall leave as soon as we can manage. John is doing much better today, and I believe he can handle the remaining journey to Attleborough."

Lawrence swallowed and blinked quickly. "Today?" he said.

She nodded. "I don't wish to worry my father if I can prevent it, and he expected us to arrive yesterday at the latest."

He suppressed a wry smile. She was going out of her way to appease her father; Lawrence was going out of his way to avoid and disappoint his.

"If you wouldn't mind terribly," she continued, "we would like to leave within the hour for town." She clenched her teeth, watching his expression.

He managed a nod, but he felt a sort of panic building inside him. He had only an hour left before he had to say goodbye to Miss Renwick. He forced himself to think on the way she had angered him yesterday—how she had reminded him of his parents.

But all he could see in front of him was the face he had come to love, the eyes he ached to make dance and twinkle, the mouth that enchanted him when it turned up in a smile or, just as captivating, tried so hard to suppress one.

THE CARRIAGE RIDE to town was surreal. Lawrence had, in an effort to cling on to whatever time was left, offered to accompany them on the ride. John chattered happily, having come to the conclusion that his injury was evidence of his courage—a badge of honor for an aspiring pirate. Anne laid on the floor, just as she had the night the Renwicks had arrived.

Miss Renwick's eyes seemed most often to rest on her hands which were clasped firmly in her lap. When her eyes did rove, they never met Lawrence's gaze.

He kept up with John's talking as best as he could, though his mind was very much elsewhere. With the Renwicks leaving and his parents descending upon him at any moment, there was no reason at all to stay at Holywell House.

The Renwick's coachman was, as promised, awaiting them in the courtyard of the inn, though their arrival coincided with Mr. Jeffers yelling at the coachman that his equipage was unwelcome if he had no paying guests. He stopped mid-sentence, though, when he saw Lawrence step out and begin speaking with the coachman, directing his own coachman to help move the Renwicks' portmanteaux over.

Before Lawrence knew it or was prepared for it, he found himself kneeling down to embrace John, with Miss Renwick standing behind her brother.

"When are you coming to visit, Lawrie?" said John.

Lawrence glanced up at Miss Renwick. Why must he always be so curious about her reaction? She had turned her head away, watching the bustle happening around them.

"I don't know." It was all Lawrence could think to say. He didn't wish to lie, but he couldn't bear to see John's face turn crestfallen if he knew that Lawrence was not going to visit.

"John," Miss Renwick said, "we should be going. We have a long day of travel ahead of us."

John nodded and called for Anne to follow him up into the carriage.

Lawrence stood, taking in a breath as he came to face Miss Renwick. What could he possibly say?

"I know you dislike being thanked," she said, "but I cannot leave without saying it."

The distance which he had felt growing between them since their confrontation in the garden suddenly vanished, and he noticed that her expression had become soft as she looked at him, her gaze direct and clear.

"Thank you for saving us, Mr. Debenham—more than once. I am sorry that I overstepped my bounds, and I hope we may part friends."

He felt the magnetic pull strengthen as he returned her gaze. The din of inn servants calling out to one another, carriage wheels and horse hooves on cobblestone—it all felt distant.

He needed to forget Miss Renwick as soon as he possibly could.

But he found himself scanning her face, trying to store up the memory of her eyes, the color of blue at dusk; her lips, the color of the pink peonies which had taken over his flower beds; her hair, the color of sweet honey.

"We will never forget your kindness," she said. She turned on her heel and ascended the carriage steps as Lawrence looked on in a daze.

He stood, rooted to the spot as he watched the carriage pull away, John's face looking at him through one of the windows.

"LEFT ALREADY?" Mr. Adley said, incredulous. "But the boy has a broken arm."

Lawrence said nothing, pouring himself a glass of ale—the only drink they had left in the house. He should have asked Mr. Jeffers for more brandy and wine when he was in town.

Mr. Adley continued, "But Miss Renwick had said only yesterday that they would likely remain through Saturday."

"But she left," Mr. Bower said in his practical voice. "Deb's just said that."

Lawrence set down his glass with more violence than he intended. "What does it matter to you? You seemed anxious enough for them to go."

Mr. Bower looked up at the clanking noise, and Mr. Adley pursed his lips before saying calmly. "I didn't think you would actually let Miss Renwick leave without making your intentions known."

Lawrence felt his mouth becoming dry. "What intentions?"

Mr. Adley threw up his hands. "Doing it much too brown, Deb! It's plain as a pikestaff you're half-mad for the girl."

"After only a few days of knowing her?" Lawrence said impatiently.

Bower was regarding him with a contemplative gaze. "Easy. Only took one breakfast with her for Adley and I to know which way the wind was blowing."

Lawrence clenched his jaw. The last thing he needed was for his friends to join ranks with his parents in convincing him to marry a responsible, respectable woman. He had assumed he would have their support. To hear them second-guess his decision irritated him beyond measure.

"Ah," he said. "I see what this is." He looked back and forth between his friends. "You've tired of my company and wish to rid yourselves of me by encouraging me to marry."

Mr. Adley slammed his hands down on the table. "Take a damper, Deb! Do you think Bower and I would be here if we had half a chance with someone like Miss Renwick? I didn't take you for such a slow top." He shook his head, stood, and walked out of the room.

Lawrence stood still, his jaw working. The anxious feeling he had been stifling underneath all his rationalization began to loom larger. He had always thought he knew his friends well—that they had no desire to marry; that they only wished to live out their lives with full stomachs, a bottomless supply of spirits, and entertainment to pass the time. Surely Mr. Adley hadn't meant what he said about wishing to marry.

"Something to say, Deb." Bower's voice cut through his thoughts.

Lawrence's brows flicked up as he noted that Bower was standing, both hands on the table, as he looked at Lawrence with a clear gaze.

"Seems you've spent your life feeling under the thumb of your father. If you only do what you know he won't like, and you don't do what he will like, well—" he raised up his shoulders in a drawn out shrug "—I don't see that you've really come out from under his thumb. Time to figure out what you want for yourself."

He looked at Lawrence a moment more as if he had more to say. "That's all," he said. He followed after Mr. Adley, patting Lawrence on the shoulder on the way out.

He had meant to talk to his friends about leaving Holywell House before his parents' arrival. But he instead sat dazedly on the wingback chair, bringing his fingers to his head and rubbing his temples. Bower's words were oddly reminiscent of what Miss Renwick had said before John's disappearance.

"I discovered that it served me better to think of my duties as opportunities rather than burdens."

He shook his head rapidly, trying to rid his mind of her image. The thought of embracing duty was foreign to him. He had been fighting it for years. But why? He had been so worried that he would fail; that his parents would be disappointed in him. But where had his fighting and fear led him? To a house in a state of disrepair, the woman he loved departed, and no prospect of any future to speak of.

He stood. It was time for change.

CHAPTER 12

*E*leanor was quiet for almost the entire ride home. John had much to say about their time at Holywell House and, more particularly, about Lawrie and when he might come visit. She began to feel as though she had the beginnings of a headache.

The roads were nearly dry, but the recent rain and equipages which had ridden over the wet dirt made for a jarring ride. Twice she had to stifle the impulse to tell John not to mention Lawrie's name again.

But mercifully, just as she thought she was at the end of her patience, John began to quiet down, his head soon slumping over onto the side of the chaise. How he could sleep with such jolting, she had no idea, but she would gladly accept the happy development.

With nothing to occupy her but her thoughts, she found herself fighting off fleeting memories of the past few blissful days at Holywell House. Images of meeting laughing eyes with Mr. Debenham countless times as John said and did outrageous things; tumbling into his arms as she attempted to "walk the plank;" the moment when they found themselves shoulder to shoulder on the bed in the Neverland room.

But the memories always ended with the controlled but angry expression Mr. Debenham had worn when he had found her in the garden.

She turned her head to look out the window at the pink-tinged sky and the sun setting on the horizon. Just as she had supposed, their time at Holywell House would soon become a distant memory, one so surreal that she would surely begin to doubt that it had happened at all.

No doubt John would insist on speaking of it for some time to come. But inevitably, in his childlike predisposition to find novel things to focus attention on, he would speak of Lawrie less and less until his name was all but forgotten.

THE FIRST FEW days at Watton Place in Attleborough were full of family and settling in. Eleanor's father had noted John's splinted arm with an anxious glance at Eleanor when they first arrived. She smiled at him to reassure him that all was well, and she noted how his shoulders seemed to relax.

Her father seemed happier at Watton Place than she had seen him in quite some time. He was often silent as the siblings enjoyed their customary banter at mealtimes, but, now and then he would join in the laughter with his own soft chuckles—something Eleanor hadn't witnessed since her mother's passing. Whatever sadness she herself might have to endure from all that had come from moving to Watton Place, her father's growing peace was surely a cost well worth it.

She found herself equally desirous and hesitant to join her siblings at every opportunity. When they were together, she wasn't plagued with memories. But she also longed for solitude—for time to explore the happiness she had felt just a few days before. Would she spend the rest of her life trying to recapture those feelings?

Three weeks after their arrival at Watton Place, Eleanor sat in the parlor, working on a particularly difficult sampler, when her father walked in. The lines on his face were beginning to deepen, and his figure was beginning to widen, but Eleanor preferred it to the gauntness which had been prevalent on his face for so long.

"I have received an invitation," he said, holding a refolded letter in his hand, "to go for a short visit to a friend of mine. He makes it clear that he would welcome any of the family who is able to come. I thought we would all go, if you are agreeable?"

Eleanor paused before answering. She liked their new home at Watton Place. It was green and lush and the home itself not long-since redecorated. But so much of the house had somehow become connected with Mr. Debenham in her mind and heart. Her first impressions had occurred at her lowest point, when she was feeling everything most intensely since leaving Holywell House.

It was a few days before she realized why her father's recovery would have suddenly begun to quicken now that he was in a new place, away from all the memories of the home he had shared with Eleanor's mother.

Eleanor recognized, though, that her options for a future expanded with every day that her father's recovery progressed. He would continue to rely on her less and less, and John seemed to have taken quickly to the tutor of his new friends at the nearby parsonage. Eleanor's father hoped that the man would agree to tutor John as well.

"Yes, I think I should like a short escape," Eleanor said to her father with a smile.

He returned the smile, coming to kiss her on top of her head. "Let us plan to leave Wednesday, then." He turned to leave the room again.

"Father?" she said, the sampler shaking slightly in her hands.

He looked at her with an expectant brow.

She took in a breath, saying, "I think I should like to go to London when the Season begins. Perhaps Aunt Margaret would still be willing to take me under her wing." She had been thinking on the possibility for a week, knowing that a come-out would be her greatest chance to make a match.

Was there love like she had felt for Mr. Debenham waiting in London? It seemed doubtful to her, but what other choice did she have?

She needed to move forward, to take charge of the future as much as she could. Otherwise she would end up as a spinster, hanging upon her father's sleeve with only the prospect of poverty when he died.

Her father smiled softly, looking at her through slightly narrowed eyes. "Let us talk on that when we've returned."

She nodded, content to let him consider the proposal. Surely he would see the wisdom in it if given the time to study the matter out.

Wednesday morning dawned sunny, with only wisps of cloud floating near the horizon. Her father had insisted on an early departure, so it was just after breakfast that the family climbed into the two carriages, leaving Watton Place behind.

Eleanor hadn't any idea which direction they would be traveling, only that it would be a few hours' ride before they arrived. She was content to be somewhere new, to be free of everything that reminded her of Mr. Debenham. Wherever they were going, perhaps it would be what she needed to steel herself and accept what never would be, embracing what still could be.

John sat across from her, and they were playing clapping games to distract John from his constant question: "How much longer do we have?"

John stopped and perked his ears up as the sound of the carriage wheels meeting a pebbled drive. Eleanor raised her brows and smiled at him as the carriage ambled on, finally coming to a stop.

"It's Holywell House!" John cried.

Eleanor froze. He must be mistaken. There were undoubtedly

dozens of estates with a similar exterior to that of Holywell House. She looked out the carriage window, and her heart stopped.

It was Holywell House.

And yet it wasn't. Gone was the ivy-covered façade, the weeds poking up from the pebbled courtyard. The overgrowth which had flanked the sides of the house was gone, now groomed and manicured. The fields which lay to the west of the house were recently harvested and tilled.

The carriage door opened, and John hopped down with Anne right behind him.

"Lawrie!" he called in exultation.

Eleanor stilled again, not daring to descend from the carriage. This must be a mistake. Her father had never mentioned whose estate they would be visiting. Why had she never thought to ask? Because she could never have fathomed that it would be Mr. Debenham he had been in communication with—a gentleman she was certain her father had no acquaintance with. Her father came to the open carriage door, looking inside with a smile.

"Why don't you come out, Nell dear?" he said, extending his hand to assist her down.

"Father," she said, her voice cracking. She cleared her throat as she extended her hand. "I don't understand."

"You will," he said, taking her hand in his and helping her down.

She looked up hesitantly and saw Mr. Debenham, crouched down next to Anne whose paws danced and whose tail wagged furiously as he pet her. He rose to a standing position, a grin plastered on his face, and his eyes turned to Eleanor. She swallowed, and his smile flickered before softening.

He walked toward Eleanor and her father, exchanging a hearty handshake with the latter who said, "I believe you two have much to discuss. We shall leave you to it." He squeezed Eleanor's hand and then walked away toward the line of servants ready to bring in the valises and portmanteaux from the carriages.

Eleanor watched her father walk off, unprepared to meet Mr.

Debenham's gaze. She knew an impulse to cry out to her father, telling him not to go. What did he expect her to say to Mr. Debenham? And how did they even come to be there?

"Miss Renwick," he said, his voice quieter than usual. "Would you care to take a walk with me through the gardens?"

Eleanor looked up at him, the memory of a pile of weeds and the harsh words that had come along with them. Why would she wish to return to such a place? But his arm was extended, and she took it, feeling it was easier than to speak her thoughts. She felt bemused by the whole situation, and she wished her father would have explained it all to her so that she didn't have to choose between guessing and asking Mr. Debenham.

They turned the corner, and Eleanor was momentarily distracted from her thoughts by the small slice of the gardens she could see from the side of the house. More came into view as they approached. All the hedges had been pruned and the flower beds weeded so that they burst with color: greens, reds, pinks, yellows, and whites. The long pool had been emptied and then filled with fresh water and then topped with lilypads.

"Oh my," she said. She saw Mr. Debenham look at her from the corner of her eye, and she chanced a glance up at him. He was looking down at her with a warmth she had never before encountered. Her cheeks began to burn, and she reached for something to say. "You have been very busy."

He let out a large sigh. "You have no idea. But Farmer Foster's help has likely halved my own trouble."

"He has been helping you?" she said, gratified to know that Mr. Debenham's relationship with the kind man should be continuing on so well.

Mr. Debenham nodded. "I've hired him on as my bailiff and let go the steward my father hired. Foster is well able to do the work I need him for. And much more qualified."

She smiled, and they came to the bench she had once sat on. No longer was there room only for one, and Mr. Debenham sat down beside her, keeping her arm in his. Eleanor stared at the pool in front of them, her eyes glazing over. Did he really mean to leave her wondering about how her family had come to be at Holywell House?

She needed to understand—her heart was too ready to open itself to Mr. Debenham, whether she gave it permission or not; too ready to accept that it had found its way back to what it wanted.

"What am I doing here?" she blurted out, still looking at the flowers. "What is my family doing here?"

"I wrote to your father, introducing myself, and I asked him to come here. To bring you." He looked at her, and she returned his glance, meeting his eyes squarely for the first time. There was something different about them; something older and more certain. She didn't want to look away until she understood it.

"Why?" she asked plainly.

"I needed to apologize," he said, staring out at the rear of the house and then surveying the grounds which were visible from the low-hedged gardens. "I should have explained things to you—I shouldn't have let you go." He raised his shoulders up and drew in a breath. "I have been fighting against my father for years, trying to establish my own life, to relieve myself of the suffocating obligation I've felt at his hands. That is why Holywell House was in such a pitiful state. I couldn't bring myself to do what he expected me to do."

He paused a moment, looking at her. "And then you came. Which leads me to the second reason I asked your father to bring you all this way. I want to thank you."

Eleanor felt her stomach drop. He brought her all this way to thank her?

"Someone I know taught me not to listen to such dull stuff," she said, her mouth turning up in a small smile.

He chuckled. "He sounds like a dashed fool. I think I will ignore his questionable advice." He turned toward her, and his smile faded, replaced with the soft look that she had seen him wear in the courtyard upon seeing her. He took her hand from his arm and placed it between his own hands. She felt her heart beat erratically.

He shook his head. "You can't know all the good that our fateful encounter has brought into my life. You showed me in a few short days how to live a more meaningful, joyful existence; how to free myself of the burden I had chosen—of feeling oppressed, I believe you phrased it. Your words and your friendship helped me to a place in mere days that I thought never to arrive at: a reconciliation with my parents."

Eleanor raised her brows, and he nodded toward the house. "They are staying under the same roof as I am, and not one of us has raised a voice or stalked out of a room—a miracle in and of itself—believe me."

She smiled weakly but turned her head away, pulling her hand from his. "Surely you realize that none of that is my doing. But even if it had been, I assure you that a letter would have sufficed."

"You've interrupted me," Mr. Debenham said with a half-smile. "I wasn't finished thanking you. And I assure you that a letter would not have sufficed for all of the things I wish to say." He smiled at her in a way that made her heart skip and then beat double time.

"As I was saying," he said in mock severity, his eyes twinkling at her, "my impromptu trip into town was the most important decision I've ever made. It brought me to you."

Eleanor blinked twice in quick succession, her chest suddenly expanding at what she was hearing. He brought one of his hands to her cheek, and she felt its warmth travel through her. The space between them seemed to slowly contract, and he raised a second hand to her other cheek, lifting his head to kiss her forehead gently.

She closed her eyes, bringing her hands to rest on his arms.

He pulled away, looking into her eyes and then down to her parted lips.

She swallowed, and he tipped her chin up with a finger, pressing his own lips to hers in a soft kiss that became more urgent and then soft again until he pulled away.

He wrapped his arms around her waist and rested his forehead against hers as she closed her eyes for a moment, trying to gather her senses.

"You bore with me," he said, "in a run-down house with no servants and a testy temper, Eleanor. Can you bear with me a while longer? Say, for the rest of your life?"

"I can't make any promises," she said, "But I should very much like to try."

She could feel his smile, matching her own, and he pulled her in more tightly against him.

"*En guarde!*" John's shouting voice met Eleanor's ears, and she pulled away from Mr. Debenham who looked toward the disruptor.

John had come running out of the French doors with a real sword in hand, but he stopped short upon seeing his intended victims. His head tilted to the side and lowered his sword. "Are you going to marry my sister, Lawrie?"

Mr. Debenham threw his head back in a laugh. "I have every intention of marrying your sister, my good man. Does that bother you?"

John shook his head. "I already knew you would. It was bellows to mend with you ever since you clapped eyes on her, wasn't it?"

Eleanor clamped her lips together to stifle a laugh and looked at Mr. Debenham who was doing his level best to suppress his own smile.

"Just so, John," he said. "Just so."

Join my newsletter to keep in touch and learn more about the Regency era! I try to keep it fun and interesting.

You can also connect with me and eight other authors in the Sweet Regency Romance Fans group on Facebook.

If you'd like to read the first chapter of the first book in the Families of Dorset Series, go ahead and turn the page.

WYNDCROSS: A REGENCY ROMANCE

CHAPTER ONE

Kate Matcham thumbed the threadbare crimson reticule sitting on her lap, feeling the reassuring presence of the letter inside. Her eyes shifted to the numerous ball guests surrounding her and her aunt Fanny.

"For heaven's sake, Fanny," she pleaded, "keep your voice down."

Nearby, Charlotte Thorpe whispered to the woman next to her, and Kate's jaw clenched. If Charlotte Thorpe overheard, all of London would know in a matter of days. Kate was already regretting telling her aunt of the letter.

Lady Fanny Hammond guiltily covered her mouth with a hand, but she couldn't dampen the excitement in her eyes. "Do you even know your stepfather's worth?" she half-whispered, leaning over in her seat toward Kate.

"No," Kate admitted, rushing on before Fanny could enlighten her, "but it is immaterial. His brother stands to inherit, and I am certain that he will be found alive and well."

It was certainly what Kate hoped would occur. It would be much easier if the choice not to accept the fortune was made for her. She smiled and inclined her head at a passing acquaintance.

"But he might well be dead," Fanny said optimistically, smiling at the same acquaintance. "People die in the West Indies quite frequently, I believe."

Kate looked down at her young aunt with a mixture of consternation and amusement. "How very morbid you are."

"Perhaps," Fanny said, her wide, blue eyes scanning the room, "but a little morbidity might not be uncalled for when twenty thousand pounds are at stake."

"Twenty thou—" Kate's eyes widened. She took a steadying breath.

Whether it was twenty pounds or twenty thousand pounds, she could never accept money from her stepfather, Mr. Dimmock. Nor did she believe he would give her the chance.

"It's neither here nor there," she said. "My stepfather detests me and always has. He would surely find a way to ensure that his fortune couldn't pass to me."

"Well," Fanny huffed, "I'm sure I don't see why. Hateful man."

Kate smiled at Fanny's offense on her behalf. She had long since ceased trying to curry favor with her stepfather. Nor did she waste energy trying to understand the dislike for her which he took no pains to hide.

Fanny continued, "I'm sure you are the most unassuming and pleasant stepdaughter one could wish for."

Kate leaned over to kiss her aunt's cheek. "And you are the most wonderful chaperone one could wish for—not to mention the most beautiful and young and charitable and long-suffering."

"The most beautiful?" Fanny said, ignoring the other epithets in favor of the one she most prized. "Do you really think so?" She touched her honey curls with a cupped hand in the gesture Kate had come to know well.

"Without question," Kate said with feigned gravity, hand over her heart. Hoping to keep Fanny's mind off the letter, she continued, "In truth, you are more in need of a chaperone than I."

Fanny scoffed. "I need no chaperone. I am a widow, besides

being fully two years older than you, my dear." She stretched herself high in her seat, though Kate's tall figure still eclipsed her.

Kate smiled and shook her head as she looked off into the groups of people dancing and conversing. The brightly lit ballroom was peppered with Fanny's admirers. "I have tried my best to keep the fortune-hunters at bay, but one can only do so much, you know." She sighed melodramatically and then turned to wink at her aunt.

Fanny collapsed her fan and rapped Kate's knuckles with it. "Nonsense," she said, but her blush-tinged cheeks betrayed the pleasure she took in flattery.

Kate spotted Mr. Walmsley on the other side of the room, making his way over to them in his characteristic waddle. "Not all of them are fortune-hunters, thankfully," Kate said pointedly.

The portly but kind-hearted aspirant to Fanny's hand was sweating profusely as he tried to navigate his way through the crowd holding two drinks. His plump figure made him look all at once older and younger than his thirty-three years.

"No," Fanny said. "Walmsley is decidedly not a fortune-hunter. He is more likely to be hunted for his own fortune, you know. But I am not at all sure if I shall accept his offer." Fanny bit her lip as she tracked his movement toward them. She turned to Kate with a conscience-stricken expression. "The truth is, I have so much enjoyed being widowed."

Kate's eyes lit up with laughter, and Fanny rushed on, "I know it is an awful thing to say, but I married so young. I never had a real Season. Naturally Lord Hammond was very good to me," she added quickly, "and I had no reason to complain of my treatment at his hands. But he preferred spending most of the year in the country."

She said the last word with a touch of revulsion and then looked around the room with an air of melancholy. "London is my home, and I'm not sure that I'm ready to give this life up all over again."

Kate could readily believe that Fanny would be loath to abandon her current lifestyle. Her schedule consisted of one social engagement after another, and her wealth and widowhood made her an object of gallantry.

Mr. Walmsley came before them, handing one drink to Fanny and the other to Kate. "Too many people here, I tell you." The skin under his chin trembled as he shook his head. "I could barely get my hands on these drinks. Was nearly obliged to call a fellow out! The jackanapes tried to cut in front of me for these last two."

"Oh dear," breathed Kate. She lowered her head and turned it to the side, hunching her shoulders and hoping to avoid the attention of the gentleman heading in their direction.

"Not to worry, Miss Matcham," Walmsley reassured her in ignorant bliss. "I didn't *actually* call him out. Only tempted me for a moment. I'm afraid my dueling days are long past. My circumference, you see, provides much too wide a target for my taste." He looked down at his belly and rubbed it with fondness.

"No, not that," Kate hissed, biting her lip to keep from laughing at Mr. Walmsley's words. But it was too late. She had been recognized. She straightened hastily in her chair, pretending that she had been picking something up, and contrived a smile at the man approaching them.

Sir Lewis Gording stopped and bowed. His thin lips were stretched in a smile, though the lines above them betrayed the slight contempt they most often wore. Had Kate been standing, she would have come eye to eye with Sir Lewis. Despite their matched height, he always managed to make her feel as though he was looking down upon her.

Unlike so many of the young women who tolerated his aggressive flirting to placate their hopeful mothers, Kate had always found his company uncomfortable and paid him only the attention that civility required. Unfortunately for her, Sir Lewis seemed to find her company more desirable as a result. He was impervious to her subtle snubs.

"Good evening, your ladyship. Walmsley." He bowed and turned toward Kate. "Miss Matcham, might I have the pleasure of the next dance?"

She groaned inside but maintained the same contrived smile of civility. Out of politeness and the desire to be a credit to Fanny, she would not refuse him, but the feeling of obligation chafed her.

"Of course," she replied, with a bow of her head.

Helping her up from her seat and tucking her hand into his arm, Sir Lewis led her away from Fanny and Mr. Walmsley. Kate turned her head back toward Fanny with a look of helplessness. Fanny smiled at her and bobbed her head up and down in encouragement, failing to recognize the distress signal.

"I've changed my mind," Sir Lewis said, and Kate whipped her head back around, afraid he had witnessed her attempted call for help. "Let us instead take a turn about the room."

Before she could respond, he had guided her away from the dance floor. They passed through two groups of chatting women, the sound of organdy, muslin, and silk skirts brushing against one another. Kate envied the merry voices of the women they passed. If only she could disappear into one of their circles. Instead she was being guided firmly toward the brocade-draped windows lining the room.

Sir Lewis was clearly used to being in control. It was part of what she so disliked in him.

"As you please, sir," she said, clenching her teeth behind her smile. She felt his eyes studying her.

"You are the picture of perfection this evening, if I may say so," he said. His eyes moved from her head down to her slippers.

Where other ladies might blush at such a high compliment, or at least at his unabashed scrutiny, Kate's nostrils flared in consternation. "I'd prefer you didn't say such things, Sir Lewis, as you well know that I'm not fond of your exaggerated compliments. Or of such compliments in general."

"Every woman loves compliments," he said with his characteristic certainty.

The retort which rose to Kate's lips was cut off as she felt a tap on her shoulder and heard a man clear his throat. She turned.

The gentleman she faced bowed slightly. When he rose to his full height, he was a few inches taller than she. His brown hair was long enough to curl but had been brushed away from his face, though a few curls seemed to be attempting a revolt. Small lines at the corners of his eyes revealed a tendency to laugh, but as he met eyes with Sir Lewis, his pleasant expression flickered.

"Sir Lewis." He nodded.

"Good evening," Sir Lewis said, raising his brows in a gesture both questioning and dismissive.

"Forgive the interruption," the gentleman said, and he smiled at Kate. "I believe this belongs to you, Miss."

He held her crimson reticule in his outstretched hand. One of the strings—evidently the one which she had wrapped around her wrist—had finally broken. "You dropped it a moment ago back there." He gestured with his head behind him.

Her eyes widened, and she looked at him with dismay. Had he seen its contents? Her arm shot out for the bag. Only when her hand reached his did she realize how peculiar her behavior would seem.

She looked up at him with warm cheeks and a sheepish smile. His brows were slightly raised, his head tilted to one side, and his eyes twinkling as he watched her reaction.

"It is indeed mine," she said, taking it from him gently with a relieved smile. "Thank you for returning it to me."

A smile played at his lips. "Yes, well, I admit that I was hard-pressed to give it up. Crimson is particularly good with my complexion, I'm told." He sighed. "But alas, it was not to be. My conscience won out in the end. I wish you joy of it."

Kate took her lips between her teeth to suppress a smile, and his eyes danced.

Sir Lewis's voice cut in on the exchange. "And now that you have returned it, we will trouble you no longer."

The gentleman's smile tightened, and he looked at Sir Lewis as if he had a rejoinder on his lips. Kate wished he would say whatever it was, but he bowed, shot another glance of shared enjoyment at her, and walked away.

Kate took a deep breath as she watched him walk off, feeling she had been undeservedly lucky. If he— (who was he? Sir Lewis had been disobliging enough not to introduce him)—had not seen her drop the reticule, who might have happened upon it? The person would have been required to look inside to determine its owner, and who knows what they might have seen, how much they would have read, or what information from the letter they would have decided to pass along to their acquaintances.

The last thing Kate wanted was for anyone else to take the letter's contents as seriously as Fanny had done.

"Where were we?" Sir Lewis said. "Ah, yes. I had just complimented your ever-increasing beauty."

Kate gripped her lips together, wishing that the interlude with the handsome stranger could have lasted longer. Any reprieve from Sir Lewis's attentions was a welcome one.

"Please don't," she said, feeling fatigued at the thought of continuing to fend off Sir Lewis.

His lopsided smile appeared again. "Would you really deprive me the opportunity of expressing the thoughts that fill my head?" His eyes were at odds with his words, almost mocking her. How many women had he flattered in the same way?

"Perhaps," said Kate, striving for a light tone, "if the thoughts are kept within they will diminish altogether in time, though I doubt they are as pervasive as you claim."

"I disagree," he said, coming to stand in front of her and blocking her way. "They demand to be given expression, Kate." He said her name slowly, looking into her wary green eyes with his cynical gray ones.

"Forgive me, sir," she said with a bite to her voice, "but I have not given you leave to call me by my given name." She moved to walk around him, but he caught her arm. She stopped but didn't turn her head to look at him. She had, in the past, done her best to put him in his place with gentle civility, but with each meeting, he seemed to grow more aggressive.

"No, perhaps you have not," he acknowledged, looking at her profile and gripping her arm with his teeth bared in a false smile. "But you will do so shortly, I feel confident."

"Your confidence is misplaced, sir," she said. She glanced at the group of people nearest them. The gentleman who had returned her reticule stood between two women. His intent gaze was on Kate.

She tore her arm from Sir Lewis's grasp, feeling a pressing need to make it plain that she was not a willing recipient of Sir Lewis's attentions. She looked back to Sir Lewis, her gaze hard and direct. "If you will excuse me," she said.

He grabbed her by the wrist and leaned in toward her. His lip turned up on one side. The smirk made her hair stand on edge. "You would have everything you could want living under my protection, you know."

She reared back, and her eyes glinted dangerously. "You dare offer such a thing to a lady?"

His smirk morphed into contempt, and the grip on her wrist tightened uncomfortably. "A lady? You are the daughter of a social climber and the stepdaughter of an unscrupulous tradesman." He blew out a derisive puff of air. "A woman with connections such as yours cannot be so particular about whom she accepts and on what terms, Kate." He drew out her name, as if to mock her.

She felt the blood rush into her cheeks, betraying her embarrassment and anger. But before she could think of a suitable reply, they were interrupted again.

"Excuse me."

Kate turned with a suppressed sigh of relief, meeting eyes with the same gentleman who had brought her reticule just minutes before.

Kate was conscious of her angry, red cheeks, and she tried to control the way her chest heaved with furious breaths. The gentleman had impeccable timing.

"I hesitate to deprive you," he said, "of the exalted company you somehow find yourself in, Sir Lewis, but I come to claim a promised dance." He wore a congenial grin, but his eyes challenged Sir Lewis.

Sir Lewis dropped Kate's wrist and looked at her as if to verify the man's claims.

She raised her brows at him in a similarly challenging gesture. She was more than happy to disregard that she had never promised the stranger a dance.

The gentleman shifted his eyes to Kate, the challenging glint gone. He wore a soft smile as he offered her his arm. She smiled at him gratefully, made a quick, icy apology to Sir Lewis, and walked away on the arm of her deliverer.

She looked up at his profile beside her. The man's expression was unreadable, and he looked straight ahead as though nothing out of the ordinary had occurred.

Kate drew in a deep breath, feeling her cheeks cool.

"Thank you," she said. Her brow creased. "Or my apologies. I'm not sure which is appropriate, to be honest."

He looked down at her with an amused tilt to his mouth. "Why should you assume either is necessary?"

"Well," she said matter-of-factly, "either you recognized my discomfort and intervened, perjuring yourself in the process, I might add; or," she shrugged, "you have mistaken me for a lady who had indeed promised you a dance, in which case I apologize for the misunderstanding and simply feel grateful that it occurred."

His smile grew. "I only did what I wish someone would do for me whenever I find myself in Sir Lewis's company."

A laugh escaped Kate. "I will endeavor to return the favor if I ever see you in his presence."

"The prospect of being in his company suddenly becomes more enticing," he said.

She glanced at him. Was he flirting with her?

But he was looking toward the dance floor where a set was forming.

"Shall we?" he said, motioning to the dancers.

Kate hesitated. She couldn't deny that the prospect of dancing with him was appealing. But they hadn't even been properly introduced.

"You realize," he said, watching her hesitation, "that if you refuse, I will have doubly perjured myself tonight. And you will bear some responsibility for the second instance."

How did he manage to look so censuring and playful at the same time? Kate suppressed a smile and shot a glance in the direction of Sir Lewis. His eyes were on them. She found that she was gripping the gentleman's arm harder than was merited and loosened her hold.

"How could I possibly refuse after such a compelling argument?" she said, looking up at him with a smile.

They took their places among the set on the dance floor for a lively country dance. She had danced with gentlemen after only a brief introduction, but never had she danced with one whose name she didn't know. The knowledge that they were complicit in defying etiquette brought a shade of pink to Kate's cheeks which had nothing to do with the heat of the room. There was something exhilarating about it all.

Her partner was skilled but droll in his dancing, and Kate found that her cheeks began to ache from smiling and laughing. There was hardly time for conversing amongst the energetic movements of the dance, and yet Kate felt carefree with her anonymous partner. His hand was light yet sure, and she felt a thrill each time the dance required them to stand shoulder to shoulder or join hands.

Before she knew it, though, the set had ended, and they were bowing to one another.

He offered her his arm, his breathless grin matching her own. "Where shall I convey you, madam? Back to Sir Lewis?"

"By all means," she said with a threatening lift to her eyebrows, "if you wish my specter to haunt you the rest of your days."

He threw his head back in a chuckle. "That prospect is not nearly as horrifying as you seem to think it."

"Well before you convey me to my aunt—" she emphasized the word and indicated Fanny whose back was turned as she conversed with Charlotte Thorpe "—perhaps I should at least know your name?"

He drew back with a scandalized expression. "When we haven't even been properly introduced? What an appalling suggestion." A smile twitched at the corner of his mouth for a moment, and he continued walking her toward Fanny.

She pulled back on his arm, preventing their progress. "Perhaps it is. But we can hardly ask someone to introduce us after they have seen us dance together. Besides, what if someone should inquire from me after you?"

He clucked his tongue, shaking his head. "What a dilemma for you."

"For me? Why only for me?"

"You have no way to know my name," he replied.

"Nor do you know mine," she countered.

"Ah." He raised a brow enigmatically. "But I will discover it, all the same."

He pulled her gently along toward Fanny who was still too occupied with Mrs. Thorpe and two other women to remark their presence.

The gentleman shot Kate a half-smile as he bowed, then leaned in and whispered, "My name is William."

And then he walked away.

Kate watched the gentleman stride off, feeling both frustrated and captivated.

"Miss Matcham?"

The voice, full of excitement and surprise, broke in on her thoughts.

She turned around to face the owner of the unfamiliar voice. A young woman stared at her with round eyes and a large grin.

Kate hadn't any idea who she was, though there was something familiar about her. With flaxen hair, rosy cheeks, and large blue eyes brought out by the lace-covered powder blue gown she wore, it was a face Kate was sure she would have remembered.

Her bewilderment must have been apparent, because the young woman laughed.

"It's me, silly! Clara. Surely you can't have forgotten?"

Confusion morphed into recognition and astonishment, and Kate's face lit up with a large smile. "Clara Crofte? But of course!"

The two embraced quickly, and a strong aroma of lavender met Kate's nose. Clara pulled away, holding Kate out at arms' length, a hand on each shoulder. "You are quite as grown up as I am," she said. "More so, I suppose, since you are older. And so very lovely. When I asked Mary Thorpe who you were, she said, 'Why, that's Miss Kate Matcham,' and I couldn't believe it. So of course I had to come to you immediately."

"I'm very grateful you did," Kate replied. "Indeed, I am in shock to be talking to you. I've often wondered about you and your family this past decade and more, and here you are in front of me after so many years. How is your family?"

"They are well, thank you. My mother is here with me tonight, though last I saw her, she was walking with Lady Carville." She scanned the room, looking for her mother. "I don't see her at the moment, and unfortunately, we cannot stay much longer. My mother is under orders from the doctor not to be to bed too late. May we call upon you tomorrow, though?"

"Yes," Kate said with enthusiasm. "Please do. I'm staying with my aunt, Lady Hammond, in Berkeley Square. We would be delighted to receive you."

Clara beamed. "Wonderful!" She glanced away and then put a hand on Kate's arm, her eyes still fixed on whatever had caught her attention. "Oh, I'm afraid you must excuse me. I see Lord Cartwright thinks I have forgotten that I promised him this dance,"— she shot him a coy glance —"but I shall see you tomorrow." She embraced Kate again, and, with a suppressed squeal of delight, left to favor Lord Cartwright with a cotillion.

Kate turned back toward Fanny with a dazed expression, excusing herself as she bumped into one of Fanny's friends.

"Good heavens, Kate," said Fanny, "you nearly knocked over poor Mrs. Orritt. So unlike you!" Her words censured Kate, but they also contained a hint of curiosity. Fanny was always quick to perceive when someone was full of news.

"Now, your ladyship," said Mr. Walmsley, with a kind smile at Kate. "I'm sure she didn't intend to knock Mrs. Orritt over, did you?" He paused, and then added as an afterthought, "Though, even if she *had* intended it, I can't say I'd have blamed her. The last time I was invited for dinner, I'm devilish sure she had the wine watered down."

Fanny waved an impatient hand at Walmsley, dismissing his hypothesis and looking expectantly at Kate.

"I'm sorry," said Kate. "I'm only distracted with surprise. Do you know who I just spoke with, Fanny?"

Fanny looked exasperated. "Well, really, Kate. With half of London here tonight, how am I to guess which one person you spoke to?"

Kate threw off her preoccupation with a shake of her head and a laugh. "Of course you could never guess. It was Clara Crofte."

Fanny looked none the wiser, staring blankly at Kate, who was obliged to provide more information. Once Fanny made the connection, Kate informed her aunt of the Croftes' plans to call the next day.

"Oh no!" said Fanny with a look of dismay. "Surely you didn't tell them they could call tomorrow? I've been promised to Lady Carville for a sennight."

"I had entirely forgotten." Kate apologized, looking deflated before perking back up. "Well, if you aren't opposed to it, I could receive them on my own?"

Fanny readily assented to the plan.

"Oh, Fanny!" Kate sat up straight in her chair. "I must ask you—"

she scanned the room "—to tell me who a particular gentleman is." She blinked rapidly. The man was nowhere to be seen.

"Who?" Fanny said, her curiosity piqued. She followed her niece's eyes around the room.

Kate's brows drew together. "I don't see him anywhere. Perhaps he left." She went up on her toes for a better view of all the ball guests. He was tall enough that it shouldn't have been difficult to find him.

"His name is William," said Kate, still surveying the crowd.

Fanny scoffed. "He and half the men in this room, I imagine."

Kate plopped down in the nearest chair, disappointed. The charm and novelty of London had long since worn off for her, but her encounter with William had made her feel lively again for the first time in longer than she could remember. How would she ever discover his identity?

ALSO BY MARTHA KEYES

Families of Dorset Series

Wyndcross: A Regency Romance (Book One)

Isabel: A Regency Romance (Book Two)

Cecilia: A Regency Romance (Book Three)

Hazelhurst: A Regency Romance (Book Four)

Phoebe: A Regency Romance (Series Novelette)

Regency Shakespeare Series

A Foolish Heart (Book One)

Other Titles:

Goodwill for the Gentleman (Belles of Christmas Book Two)

Eleanor: A Regency Romance

AFTERWORD

Thank you so much for reading *Eleanor!* If you enjoyed the book, please leave a review on Amazon and Goodreads and tell your friends. Authors like me rely on readers like you to spread the word about books you've enjoyed.

If you would like to stay informed about my upcoming releases and other wonderful sweet romance books, sign up for my newsletter. You can connect with me on Facebook and Instagram as well. I'd love to hear from you!

Lastly, I do my best to research and understand the Regency time period as well as possible as I write my stories. If I have gotten some details wrong, I apologize. I continue learning and researching while trying to craft stories that will be enjoyable to readers like you.

ACKNOWLEDGMENTS

So much time and work has gone into the stories that I write—something that is only possible with the wonderful support I've received from family, friends, and the writing community.

Thank you to my husband, Brandon, for putting up with countless nights of me at the computer; for taking care of the boys when I am itching to get some writing in; and for supporting me in every way with my dreams, as crazy as they sometimes are.

Thank you to my boys who, while they are too young to understand what I'm working on, motivate me to be a better mother and a more well-rounded woman. They have sacrificed time with me in order for this all to come about, and they teach me so much about love with how forgiving they are.

Thank you to my mom, Karen, who is always my first reader and my biggest cheerleader; my dad, Cory, who believes in me more than I believe in myself; and my sister, Anna, who is a veritable fount of writing knowledge—who first pushed me to do NaNoWriMo.

And lastly, thank you to all my fellow Regency authors and to the wonderful communities of The Writing Gals and LDS Beta Readers. I would be lost without all of your help and trailblazing!

ABOUT THE AUTHOR

Martha Keyes was born, raised, and educated in Utah—a home she loves dearly but also dearly loves to escape whenever she can travel the world. She received a BA in French Studies and a Master of Public Health, both from Brigham Young University.

Word crafting has always fascinated and motivated her, but it wasn't until a few years ago that she considered writing her own stories. When she isn't writing, she is honing her photography skills, looking for travel deals, and spending time with her husband and children. She lives with her husband and twin boys in Vineyard, Utah.

Printed in Great Britain
by Amazon

38181796R00078